Land of Hope

MERIDIAN LINES

(INCORPORATED)

LANDING CARD

(THIRD CLASS PASSENGERS)

Manifest Sheet No. *10*

Name *Rebecca Levinsky*

List Number *6*

When landing at New York this card to be pinned to the coat or dress of the passenger in a prominent position.

Bei Ankunft in Amerika muss diese Karte gut sichtbar an der Kleidung auf der Brust oder am Hut befestigt werden.

Když cestující dorazí do přístavu v New Yorku, af má tento lístek na viditelném místě na svých šatech připečněný

Keď cestujúci dorazí do prístavu v New Yorku, nech má tento listok viditeľne pripevnený na svojích šatách.

Podczas wyladowania w Nowym-Yorku pasazerowie powinni przypiąć tą kartę do palta lub sukni na wydatnym miejscu

Pri iskrcavanju u New Yorku ova se karta mora izložiti na istaknutom mjesty na kaputu ili haljini.

При высадкѣ на берег в Нью-Іоркѣ пассажиры должны прикололоть эту карту на видном мѣстѣ к пальто или платью.

ווען איהר קומט אן אין ניו יארק מוזעגעם צו דיעזען קארטען גוט זיכטבאר אייער איהר באפעסטל אדער קלייד אויף אן אנגעזיכטענעם פלאץ.

ELLIS ISLAND

Land of Hope

✦ ✦ ✦

JOAN LOWERY NIXON

BANTAM BOOKS
NEW YORK • TORONTO • LONDON • SYDNEY • AUCKLAND

*In loving memory
of my maternal grandparents
Mathias Louis Meyer,
who came to the United States from Luxembourg,
and Harriet Louise Prien Meyer*

LAND OF HOPE

A Bantam Book / November 1992

*The Starfire logo is a registered trademark of Bantam Books, a
division of Bantam Doubleday Dell Publishing Group, Inc.
Registered in U.S. Patent and Trademark Office and elsewhere.*

Library of Congress Cataloging-in-Publication Data

Nixon, Joan Lowery.
    Land of hope/Joan Lowery Nixon.
      p.   cm.—(Ellis Island)
    *Summary: Rebekah, a fifteen-year-old Jewish immigrant
arriving in New York City in 1902, almost abandons her
dream of getting an education when she is forced to work
in a sweatshop.*
    ISBN 0-553-08110-1
    [1. Emigration and immigration—Fiction. 2. Jews—Fiction.
3. New York (N.Y.)—History—1898–1951—Fiction.] I. Title.
II. Series: Nixon, Joan Lowery. Ellis Island.
PZ7.N65Lan 1992
[Fic]—dc20   92-2769
                                                CIP
                                                AC

Published simultaneously in the United States and Canada

*Bantam Books are published by Bantam Books, a division of Ban-
tam Doubleday Dell Publishing Group, Inc. Its trademark, con-
sisting of the words "Bantam Books" and the portrayal of a
rooster, is Registered in U.S. Patent and Trademark Office and in
other countries. Marca Registrada. Bantam Books, 666 Fifth Ave-
nue, New York, New York 10103.*

PRINTED IN THE UNITED STATES OF AMERICA

BVG   0 9 8 7 6 5 4 3 2 1

CHAPTER ONE

❖ ❖ ❖

U NDER the dark shelter of the trees Rebekah
Levinsky and her family waited, scarcely
breathing, willing themselves to ignore the bitter
frost-damp chill of the night air. A pale scrap of
moon shed just enough light to illuminate the broad,
exposed strip of timber-cut field that cut across the
heavily forested land. Centering the strip, a square
of yellow light marked the roadside shack of the
border guards who patrolled to keep travelers without passports—especially Russian Jews, who were
denied passports—from illegally crossing over from
Hungary into Austria.

Eight-year-old Sofia's small hand trembled within
Rebekah's grasp, and Rebekah bent to comfort her,
even though she was every bit as frightened as her
sister.

"We've been waiting such a long time," Sofia
complained.

"Hush!" Their mother's voice exploded in a sharp
hiss of fear. Although Leah stood tall and solid, her
face unlined, her dark hair smooth under her kerchief, her voice betrayed her true feelings.

"It's all right, Leah," mumbled Elias, Rebekah's father. "Here he comes now."

Rebekah looked from her father, small-boned and gentle, to the stocky, heavy-jowled Ukranian guide who strode toward them.

There was a rustle of movement as Rebekah's older brothers, Jacob and Nessin, moved forward. Rebekah's grandfather, Mordecai Levinsky, not much taller than she, squeezed close and clasped her right hand. Others in their group clustered more tightly together—all of them neighbors who had made the hard decision to abandon their homes in the shtetl.

Rebekah knew the year 1902 had begun badly for all of them. In early February more than thirty thousand young Jewish socialists had been arrested after they rebelled against the czar's increasing control over student organizations. During this past month, April, starving peasants had looted landowners' farms in Poltava and Kharkov, and the head of the Russian secret police had been assassinated. Czar Nicholas, furious with the uprisings and determined to discourage any further revolts among the peasantry, had sent his army to retaliate. It had done so, not only in the cities, but also in the small Jewish towns whose citizens had long been victims of the dreaded pogroms—rampages in which soldiers destroyed entire towns and villages and slaughtered their residents.

Two years before, Rebekah's Uncle Avir had left for the United States against his family's advice. Her grandfather repeated what he'd read in an Orthodox journal, which warned Jews to remain in their native land rather than travel to the United States, the new country of "lies and vain dreams."

In spite of Mordecai's concerns, Avir and his wife, Anna, had emigrated. In his letters home Avir had raved to his father and brother about the freedom and opportunities in America, and on occasion he had even sent money. "Come to the United States for a life without fear," he'd urged. "Anna and I constantly worry about your safety."

Finally, when the soldiers struck in a shtetl not more than a day's journey from their own, where cousins of Leah's barely escaped with their lives, Mordecai consulted with Elias, then announced, "It is time to leave. We have no other choice."

Elias sold what he could of the family's belongings, pooled his meager savings with his father's, and purchased seven steamship tickets. The least expensive, in steerage class, cost twenty-seven American dollars apiece! It was hard for Rebekah to imagine that much money.

Now, Rebekah watched as their guide approached. He bent his neck, peering from under his eyebrows, and kept his voice low as he told them in Yiddish, the language they all spoke, "The guards want more money."

Leah answered quickly, not meeting his eyes. "We have nothing to spare. We must keep enough to pay for our train fares to Hamburg."

"And food!" Herman Mostel added. Herman had run a shop in the shtetl, but had decided to leave it all behind. "It's a long journey to Hamburg. We must eat along the way."

"I can do only so much for you. If you want to cross into Austria . . ." Moshe, as the guide called himself, shrugged and let his sentence drift into the silence.

Rebekah tucked a strand of long, dark hair under her kerchief and hugged her loose, padded jacket more tightly around her shoulders. The lumps in the lining, where her mother had sewn the family's travel money, pressed against her hips.

Mordecai, who had been gathering tidbits of information like a squirrel hoarding for winter, had learned about the guides and the way they operated. Guides were a necessity for anyone who wanted to escape Russia, but the guides consistently tried to cheat those fleeing even though they'd already overcharged. It was likely, Rebekah thought, that the Austrian border guards to whom Moshe referred had either been sufficiently bribed or were filled with the vodka Moshe had brought with him and were sound asleep. Whatever Moshe gained from this ruse would go into his own pockets.

Leah fumbled through a deep pocket in her full skirt and pulled out a handful of coins, thrusting them at the guide. Then, as they had planned, others in the group did the same. "This is all we have to give you," Leah snapped.

Squinting in the darkness to examine the pile of money, Moshe seemed satisfied. He straightened and the coins disappeared into folds in his long, thick coat as he beckoned the group to follow.

Shouldering their bundles, the refugees crossed the open land, stumbling over tree stumps and dying roots, rough stubble and deeply pocked earth, running faster and faster until they reached the shelter of the forest. Mordecai, whose right leg had been stiffened by a childhood accident, tried to keep up but limped after them, arriving out of breath. Huddled together, the travelers turned to Moshe for reassurance.

"Stay within the forest until you're out of sight of the border guards' hut," Moshe cautioned. "Then make your way toward the road. Just a few miles from here you'll come to the town of Brody." He paused and smiled before he turned to leave. "You're in Austria now, far from the Russian cossacks."

Nessin let out a whoop and beat Jacob on the shoulders, and Leah and the other women began to cry with happiness, hugging their children and one another.

They were no longer in Russia. Now they had come to this moment, Rebekah's own thoughts were so muddled she could no longer cry. She ached for all the treasures of her fifteen years of life, which she was now leaving forever. What would she do without her best friend, Chava, and her other friends in Ostrog, the place in which she had always lived?

She had often walked with her mother down the twisted cobblestone streets from their house to the marketplace, swinging a basket that soon became heavy with Leah's purchases. Rebekah loved the noise of the market as peasant farmers and peddlers arrived with vegetables, livestock, hats, shoes, clothing, lamps, and trinkets to see and buy.

"Rebekah, Rebekah, don't stop so often to gawk," Leah would tease. "There's nothing here you haven't seen before."

Sometimes on Saturdays in the afternoon peace of Shabbas while their parents were napping, Rebekah and Chava would wander through town, past the small shop where Elias worked as a tailor and past the butcher shop presided over by Chava's father.

They'd sneak quick looks at young men and women, who were dressed in their finest for the afternoon stroll, and giggle over matches that might be made.

Only last summer Chava had said, "Soon it will be our turn."

"Not that soon!" Rebekah had answered. "We are only fourteen."

Chava's eyes had sparkled as she grinned. "It's a short time between fourteen and seventeen—less than three years. Already my brother Shaul has his eye on you."

Rebekah's face had burned with embarrassment. She had already begun to wonder which young man her parents might choose when it came time to arrange her marriage—what girl wouldn't?—but she had never given a thought to Shaul, a shy, quiet man who worked with his father in the butcher shop. Why, Shaul had rarely spoken to her. Rebekah pushed the idea from her mind. Who knew what might happen in three years?

Rebekah loved to stroll down to the river, which wound through town like a curled ribbon, shimmering at the doorsteps of the rough houses that huddled near the water and rippling gently through fields and rolling hills before it disappeared into the woods. It was there, by the river, where just a few weeks ago, Rebekah had tearfully told Chava that her family was moving to America.

"Why are you leaving?" Chava had demanded. "Your father is doing well in Ostrog as a tailor. How does he know what will happen to him—to all of you—in a strange country?"

It was hard for Rebekah to understand as well. Life in her own shtetl was always so peaceful, no matter what was happening in far-off places whose names had meant nothing to Rebekah until now. She could only repeat to Chava what she had heard her father and grandfather say again and again.

"My father and grandfather are afraid of what the czar might do next. They are sure there will be more pogroms, and the cossacks could be sent to destroy Ostrog. If we don't leave we may lose everything—even our lives."

Desperately, Rebekah clutched Chava's hands and begged, "Come with us, Chava! You and your family! I'll ask my father to talk to yours and convince him to take his family to America, too!"

Chava hunched her shoulders, hugging her arms in misery. "He wouldn't listen. His cousin Abram, who left Moscow six months ago, is already in America. He has urged Papa to leave, but he won't. He insists that this is the home we have always known, and no one will take it from him." Her lower lip trembled as she added, "Ostrog is your home, too, Rebekah."

It was painful for Rebekah to speak. "I have no choice, Chava. My father has decided to leave. We must go."

"All our lives we have been best friends," Chava had cried. "I thought we would be friends forever."

"We'll still be!" Rebekah had protested, but Chava had shaken her head.

Chava's next words had come slowly and with great effort. "Only in our thoughts. Oh! Rebekah, we'll never see each other again!"

Rebekah and Chava hugged each other and sobbed.

Rebekah's throat tightened as she remembered, and her eyes burned. She tried to think of other

7

things: her loving dog, Cossi, who had been too old to make the trip and had found a home with Chava; the warm feather bed she had snuggled in with her sister Sofia on cold winter nights; the huge fireplace at the center of the house that drew the family together both for warmth and for lessons.

Her grandfather had become a well-read man, educated beyond many university students, because he could not do physical labor. His knowledge of the Talmud and literature was well known. He was eager to share it all.

Rebekah loved Mordecai's lessons. She delighted in the ease with which she had learned to speak and read in Yiddish, which was spoken in the Levinsky home, as well as Russian and English. She treasured her grandfather's praise.

"You should have been a boy," Mordecai often told her, his broad smile adding crinkles to his weathered cheeks and chin, and his dark eyes sparkling. "What a fine scholar you would have made."

Rebekah had fought back the jealousy that rose like sour milk in her throat. Grandfather was right! She *should* have been a boy! Although her brother Jacob, at seventeen, was quiet and intent in his religious studies, spending hours over the Torah, he was not interested in many other worldly subjects and did poorly in mathematics. Sixteen-year-old Nessin was even less a scholar. Full of mischief and practical jokes, he couldn't consider a serious subject for more than a minute or two. Rebekah knew she was brighter and quicker than her brothers, but she was a girl, so an education beyond that which her grandfather could give her was out of the question. She knew that in Moscow there were girls who went to school, but they weren't Jewish and they were of the nobility.

Now, here in the forest, Mordecai put his arm around Rebekah's shoulders, and she leaned against him, grateful for his teaching and his love. "We will soon be in America, Grandfather." She chose to speak in English. That would be her new mother tongue. She was surprised at the rush of fear that shivered through her body.

"Not *America,* the *United States,*" Mordecai gently corrected her. "We'll soon live in the land of hope."

Hope. Rebekah clung to the promise. *All they had left was hope.*

"Enough talk," Herman said. "We must stay here no longer. We must continue."

Herman moved into the forest, leading the way, and the others followed. Rebekah realized that they were walking more quickly, as though their bundles had become lighter, and she wondered if their fear hadn't weighed more than their possessions.

Like the other refugees, the Levinskys had packed only the things they could carry. Elias had trundled his sewing machine in a small wheeled cart so that as soon as possible he could continue his trade as a tailor. Leah had bundled up her precious goose-feather comforters and pillows and strapped them to Jacob's and Nessin's backs. Grandfather Mordecai clutched a wicker basket that contained the family's legal certificates, his books, the ram's horn he blew on Rosh Hashanah and Yom Kippur, siddur and tallis for each of the men, and Leah's treasured family recipes.

Nessin carried a tightly bound case in which were

9

packed a dozen silver forks, knives, and spoons, an ornamented silver kiddush cup, a menorah, and a pair of silver candlesticks. The bundles of clothing that Leah, Rebekah, and Sofia had slung across their backs contained both their workday clothes and their most beautiful hand-embroidered blouses and skirts, neatly folded and ready to be worn upon the family's arrival in the United States.

Their journey by train across Austria and Germany seemed interminable, and Rebekah's excitement about going to the United States turned to numb exhaustion. She tried to hide the embarrassment and humiliation she felt as each family was questioned, quarantined, undressed, and even disinfected by strangers who processed the refugees. The authorities kept saying, "Hurry along. You will miss the train. Hurry. You will miss the ship. Hurry . . . Hurry . . . Hurry!"

CHAPTER TWO

❖ ❖ ❖

"How much more must we go through?" Rebekah asked her father as the Levinskys were herded off the train in Hamburg, Germany, and into yet another long line at the docks. Ahead she could see the stacks of an enormous steamship, and her heart pounded. "Why can't we just board the ship?"

A tall, lean man wearing an official-looking uniform stopped as he heard her words, glared down at Rebekah, and answered in Yiddish, "Do you think this is pleasant for us? Not at all! But it's necessary. When immigrants arrive in the United States they are examined at Ellis Island, and if there is a problem they are returned."

"Returned?" Elias echoed.

Rebekah gasped. She had never imagined that anyone would be turned away.

"Yes, returned," the man said to Elias. "The steamship companies, at their own cost, must take the rejected passengers back to their point of origin. But will they accept this cost alone? Oh, no. They have involved the Prussian railway authorities."

"I don't understand," Elias told him. "How does this affect us? Is there something we should do?"

11

The official tossed his head impatiently. "You must go through this extra examination, which means more work for all of us. With a supervisor from the United States consul at our sides, we must examine and check and make sure that every emigrant has his ticket to the United States and the thirty dollars that is required to enter the country. You do have your thirty dollars apiece, don't you?"

"Oh, yes," Elias assured him.

Rebekah listened quietly to every word the official said, but when he turned to leave she clutched her mother's arm and asked, "Why are people turned away in America?"

Leah didn't answer, and Rebekah saw her own fear reflected in her mother's eyes.

Mordecai gently rested a hand on Rebekah's arm. "Do not worry, little one. The United States government does not want to take in people who have mental illness or contagious diseases, or people who cannot care for themselves and will need the government to support them. We have no reason to fear."

"We passed the examination at Ruhleben," Leah said, her voice trembling a bit. She tried to smile reassuringly at Rebekah.

Rebekah had heard her parents speak of Ellis Island and knew that it was the entry point to the United States for most immigrants, but when she tried to visualize the place all she could see in her mind was an island that looked like some of the river islands she had seen from the train—small, forested plots with water lapping at their eroding shores.

As Rebekah tried to imagine what Ellis Island must be like, a sudden commotion broke out just ahead of the Levinskys. Herman's wife, Hava, shrieked in terror and began to sob. "I can't go back!" she screamed. "I can't! I will die!"

"What is it? What has happened?" Elias called out, and questions began to buzz down the line like the swarms of mayflies that darted in small black clouds around the docks.

Herman, tears streaking his face, staggered from the line, his arms wrapped around his wife's shoulders as he struggled to support her and lead her away from the officials. "It is her eyes," he cried. "Trachoma!"

"I will go blind!" Hava wailed through her sobs.

"What is trachoma?" Sofia whimpered.

Leah's own face was wet with tears as she answered, "I have seen Hava rubbing and rubbing her eyes, but no one thought . . . The air was dry . . . Maybe spring pollen . . . Her mother gave her an ointment to use. Hava told me about it. Who could have known?"

The line moved forward fairly quickly, but Rebekah found it difficult to pick up her feet, which had become numb stumps of wood. It was hard work to move her head, to use her arms, to breathe, to think.

Suddenly, Elias stood before the table, across from a man dressed as a ship's officer. "Name?" the official demanded in German. "Age? . . . Native country? . . . Occupation? . . . Destination?" There were other questions, which Mordecai translated and Elias answered as the man wrote them on one line on a double page, filling in the form.

"Next," he shouted, and Mordecai edged Leah forward. Her voice trembled as she answered the

13

questions for herself and Sofia, but she was soon passed on to an inspector who wore a white coat, and Rebekah's brothers were questioned.

Rebekah stood on tiptoe, trying to study this man in the white coat. Was he the one who had refused to allow Hava to go to the United States? She shivered, aching for Hava and her husband, dreading what the man might tell Rebekah's own family.

The officer called for the next in line, and Rebekah reluctantly stepped forward. *"Ihren Namen, bitte,"* he barked at her.

Rebekah could only stare. She opened her mouth, but no words formed in her mind. To be sent back . . . how horrible!

The official spoke again, this time in Yiddish. "Do you speak Yiddish?" he asked. "Do you understand what I'm asking you?"

"I—I—" Rebekah began.

The official turned to Mordecai. "Is the girl a simpleton?" he demanded.

A simpleton? Before Mordecai could respond, Rebekah's head snapped back, and she answered angrily, "I understand you, sir. I also speak Russian and English. I will be glad to answer your questions in any of these languages."

His eyebrows rose in surprise, and a whisper of a smile twitched at one corner of his mouth as he dipped the point of his pen in an inkwell. "We can begin when you tell me your name," he said.

"Rebekah Levinsky," she answered.

She watched as he wrote it: *Rebecca.*

"That is not how my name is spelled," Rebekah protested.

"This is the way I've seen it written," he said. "Next, what is your age?"

"You mean that's how it's spelled in the United States?"

"Yes, in the United States. Age?"

"Fifteen."

"Country of origin ... Russia," he mumbled as he wrote.

Rebekah answered his questions and watched him fill the line beside her name on the list of the ship's passengers, but her mind was on the strange new spelling of her given name. *Rebecca*. She was going to the United States. She would never see her homeland again, and she couldn't even take her own name with her?

But it was Mordecai's turn to be questioned, and Rebekah had to move on before she could say anything more. The man in the white coat stepped up and looked in Rebekah's throat. Then, with a fat thumb, he pulled down her lower eyelids and nodded approval.

Mordecai joined them and said with a broad smile, "We are on our way to the United States. No one will stop us now."

With Mordecai leading the way, the Levinskys picked up their bundles and baggage and followed directions toward a large building where they had been instructed to wait until it was time to board the ship.

As they walked to the steamship company's building, clusters of men shouted at them and jostled them, offering to sell food and discounted steamship tickets or to exchange money at top rates.

Leah spoke softly. "Maybe they do give better rates, and we should take advantage of their offer."

"I have heard of these offers of so-called better rates," Mordecai answered. "They are not better. These men will cheat us. We can save our rubles for the United States."

"But they spoke in Yiddish," Leah said. "They are like us."

A corner of Mordecai's mouth turned up, but he spoke seriously. "Crooks speak any language—even Yiddish."

It seemed to Rebekah that her family had met no one but crooks and thieves all along the way. Would it be like this in America? Or would Uncle Avir find them a good place in which to begin a better life?

Until now, Rebekah had imagined that her new home in the United States would be much like the home she had left in Ostrog, except that it would be safely far away from the persecution of the czar and his cossacks. But from the time she and her family had crossed the Austrian border, through Ruhleben and Hamburg, Rebekah had seen nothing that was familiar to her. She had left forever her life in the shtetl, and she could no longer begin to imagine what sort of life awaited her in the United States of America. All she had left was her sense of hope.

CHAPTER THREE

❖ ❖ ❖

A FTER an exhausting, sleepless night during which the Levinskys crowded into a small space with hundreds of other passengers, the emigrants began to board the ship.

Formed into lines and led to the dock at which the ship was moored, everyone clustered tightly together. The air on the dock reeked of oil and fish and unwashed bodies, and Rebekah was eager to reach the deck of the ship and the chance of a fresh breeze.

She tilted her head back and glanced at the two upper decks, where passengers had already congregated. Two women wearing large hats and fashionable ankle-length coats with nipped-in waists leaned on the upper rail and watched the parade of emigrants. Rebekah studied their clothing. Elegant faceted black buttons glinted in the sunlight, next to a trim of braid. Papa, with his expert tailoring skills, could easily make coats every bit as pretty as those.

One of the women giggled and pointed. As the other laughed, Rebekah's cheeks flushed a dark red. These women were dressed very differently from the women on the docks, who had kerchiefs covering their hair instead of hats and heavy shawls around

17

their shoulders instead of coats. *The fashionable women had no right to make fun of the others,* Rebekah thought.

Rebekah noticed that a girl nearby was studying her. She smiled and asked in Yiddish, "Where are you from in Russia?"

The girl shrugged, spoke a few words in a language that Rebekah didn't understand, and turned away.

Never mind, Rebekah told herself, but her thoughts turned to Chava and her loss of her best friend. She had to fight back tears.

"Look, Mama!" Sofia cried. "Look at the people on the top deck of the ship. That's where I want to go so I can see everything!"

Mordecai smiled and tweaked one of Sofia's braids. "You will see enough from the lower deck," he said.

"But I will see more on top," she persisted.

"People who have a great deal of money have cabins on the top decks of the ship. That is called *first class,*" he explained. "People who can afford to pay more than steerage, but not as much as first class, buy cabins on decks below theirs. That is called *second class.* We will be below them in steerage."

Sofia's lower lip curled out. "I just want to go to the top for a few minutes."

"There are rules," Mordecai said. "Second-class passengers may not go into first-class territory, and steerage passengers must not go above the main deck."

"It doesn't matter," Rebekah hurried to tell her little sister. "We will all be on the same ship. We'll see the same ocean and the same seabirds. Maybe even whales!"

As the crowd arrived at the first gangplank, people began frantically to press forward, almost knocking Rebekah off her feet. Terrified, she clung to Sofia and to Mordecai, grateful when Nessin swung in behind them to block the pressure or even butt away a too-persistent encroacher.

Shoved and pummeled by countless elbows and knees, the Levinskys reached the deck and found themselves being pushed along a corridor made by two rows of the ship's sailors to an open hatchway. Leading down from the hatchway was a steep stairway into the dank hold, which was lit only by a few lanterns. There Rebekah could see narrow rows of double-decked bunks stacked close together. The first steerage passengers who had descended had staked their claims on some of the bunks and were shouting and pushing others away in an attempt to keep the beds.

Leah stopped in alarm halfway down the stairway. The onrushing tide of bodies nearly swept over her and she tripped, so that only her grip on the railing kept her from falling.

Nessin, his eyes gleaming, jumped into the swarming confusion below. He found bunks together and pushed the members of his family into them to save their places. Occasionally Rebekah heard him shout gleefully, "These beds are ours! Move on!"

As water trickles from a broken pitcher after the first rush, so the flood of bodies eventually slowed. Rebekah's heart stopped pounding, and she took time to look around. Small, salt-encrusted portholes lined each side of the hold but—even if they hadn't been so filthy—they were much too high to be able to see through.

From her perch on a top bunk, Rebekah began trying to count the number of beds but gave up after overhearing a crewman remark that there would be nine hundred passengers altogether in steerage after the ship picked up a second group of emigrants.

A second group? Rebekah wondered. *How could there possibly be room for any more?*

The noise grew, bouncing echoes across the hold, and Rebekah held her hands over her ears to cut off the deafening babble. But all sound ceased when a ship's officer called for attention and shouted instructions. There was a room with toilets and wash basins at each end of the hold. The prow for men, the stern for women. He repeated himself in four languages. Prow and stern? Rebekah wondered which end was which.

Supper would be ladled out from kettles, the officer explained, and while the weather was fair, these kettles would be positioned on the main deck. Every passenger would be issued a plate, bowl, cup, knife, fork, and spoon, and each passenger would have the responsibility of cleaning them and keeping them in a safe place between meals so they would not be lost. Steerage passengers would be welcome on the main deck only. During rough weather, however, they must remain in the hold, and the hatches would be bolted shut—for the passengers' own protection. The voyage would take close to three weeks, including the stop in Liverpool.

Rebekah knew that Liverpool was in England. She had thought that England was a prosperous country.

She spoke aloud to herself in English. "Why would English citizens need to emigrate?"

"They won't be English. They'll be mostly Irish," a voice answered carefully in a rhythmic accent Rebekah hadn't heard before. She turned to see a tall girl near her own age, seated across from her on the next bunk. The girl's hair, as pale as a new moon in winter, lay in a single thick braid down her back, nearly reaching her waist.

"They'll be Irish," the girl repeated. "I'm from Sweden. What country are *you* from?"

"Russia," Rebekah said and smiled. "I'm sorry. I didn't mean to . . . to stare." She stumbled over the word, then added, "I was talking to myself and was surprised at getting an answer."

The girl nodded. "I talked to myself a lot when I was learning to speak English. It's a hard language to learn, and I know I make lots of mistakes, but my father said we would have to arrive in the new world well prepared."

"My grandfather taught me," Rebekah said. "But he didn't insist, because I really wanted to learn to speak the language." Afraid that she had sounded like a *gantser knaker*—a know-it-all—she quickly added, "My name is Rebekah Levinsky."

For just an instant the girl gave Rebekah an appraising look, then smiled and said, "I'm Kristin Swensen. I'm sixteen—almost seventeen. How old are you?"

"I'm fifteen—almost sixteen."

Rebekah glanced in the direction of a tall, blond couple who stood in the aisle with their backs to their bunks, looking as though they were guarding their daughter. People tended to move quickly past the man, who was large-boned and muscular. "Are those your parents?" she asked.

"Yes," Kristin said.

"My parents are with me, too," Rebekah said, "and my two older brothers, and my little sister, and my grandfather."

Tears suddenly welled in Kristin's eyes. "You have such luck!" she said. "I had to say good-bye forever to my grandmother. I love her so much, and I know I'll never see her again."

As Kristin's tears spilled over, Rebekah quickly climbed across to the other bunk and searched the pocket of her skirt for a clean handkerchief. "I'm sorry," she said. "I didn't mean to say anything to make you unhappy."

Kristin had found her own handkerchief in the pocket of a full, gray skirt that was similar to Rebekah's brown one, and she blew her nose loudly. "It's not your fault," she answered. Rebekah could hear the resentment in Kristin's voice as she glared at her father and muttered, "It's *his*. He's the one who decided we should go."

"If you were in danger . . ."

"We were in no danger. We had a farm, our friends, uncles and aunts and cousins . . . and my grandmother. But a man from our village came back from the United States to visit his family, and from him my father heard about the great opportunities in the New World. All my father could talk about was the vast land to be had in the northern United States, with forests and lakes and acres of farmland to plow."

"You don't have these things in your country?"

"Of course we do! My mother reminded him of

this, and she cried and cried at leaving her sisters and her mother, but my father had made up his mind to emigrate, and so we must go to a place called Minnesota." She glanced again at her father, then back to Rebekah. "It's not fair that men make all the decisions," she whispered.

Rebekah didn't know how to answer. "The father is head of the household," she said, "but my mother has taught me that a good wife learns to gently guide her husband."

"My mother is a good wife," Kristin snapped, "but all she could do was pack her favorite belongings and follow my father." She leaned close to Rebekah and smiled like a conspirator. "What I have to tell you is true. Do you know that one day soon in the United States women will be able to vote? Already, women in America have some rights. In four Western states women already can vote for *all* offices—even president."

"They can vote? Are you sure?"

"I'm positive."

Rebekah could hardly believe this. Jews in Russia could only vote for local councils. No one voted for the czar; he was the ruler without question.

Rebekah had never even thought of such possibilities, and she was shocked. "At home the men elected the local council for our shtetl. They knew the men who wanted these government positions and if they were honest or not. They didn't need the women to vote, too."

"Why not?" Kristin asked. "I don't believe for one minute that women aren't as intelligent as men."

Sofia climbed up to join Rebekah and Kristin. "I

don't like this ship," she said in Yiddish. "It stinks so bad it makes me sick! What could be worse?"

A ship's horn blasted so loudly that Sofia shrieked and clapped her hands over her ears. Then, with a grinding roar that set Rebekah's teeth on edge, the ship's motors began to turn, and the ship—vibrating and thumping—chugged away from the dock. Rebekah shouted, "*This* could be worse!"

As Sofia buried her head in Rebekah's lap, Rebekah and Kristin looked solemnly at each other. "We're on our way," Rebekah shouted.

"Yes," Kristin said softly, and again her eyes glittered with tears.

Rebekah grabbed Kristin and Sofia's hands in hers. "Let's go up on deck!" she cried. "We can watch the ship leave the harbor!"

The girls scrambled past the others and raced up the steps to the deck's rail.

The ship was being pushed by small tugboats away from the dock, and Rebekah watched the crowded, pointed-roofed buildings of Hamburg slowly growing smaller and farther away. She squeezed Sofia's hand. "There!" she said. "You can see everything, just as you wanted to."

Sofia turned, craning her neck to look up to the top decks. "Can I see as much as that lady with the flowers on her hat?" she asked in Yiddish.

"Of course," Rebekah answered in English.

"What did your sister say?" Kristin asked.

"She asked if she could see as much as a woman on the top deck," Rebekah answered, and to Sofia she said, "Be polite. Speak English."

"English is hard. I want to speak Yiddish," Sofia complained.

Rebekah didn't reply, because she and Kristin had automatically twisted to look upward, too.

"We could have traveled in second class," Kristin said, "and my grandmother wanted us to, but my father decided to use as little money as possible for travel so that he could use most of his savings to buy land."

She sighed. "I have to keep reminding myself that in the United States *we* will have choices, not just the men in our families."

Choices? Rebekah thought. *What kinds of choices was Kristin so concerned about?*

Kristin suddenly smiled. "Let's play a game. If you had all the choices in the world, what would you choose first? Tell me, then I'll tell you."

"What would I choose first?" The words didn't come from her conscious mind, but from a deep, burning, hidden place within her heart. "I would choose," she said slowly, "to study at a great university." Rebekah was amazed at what she heard herself saying.

Kristin stared at her. "You really mean it," she said. "I thought we would say silly things, like, 'I would choose a dozen handsome, wealthy men as husbands—one at a time.' But your choice is something you really want."

"Yes," Rebekah said. She felt herself blushing, and she looked down at the tops of her scuffed boots. "But my wish is only a wish, nothing I could ever have. I will work in the home with my mother, and in two or three years my parents will arrange a marriage for me. What chance would I have to go to school?"

"Every chance. In the United States there is schooling for everyone—girls as well as boys."

"You mean little children, don't you?"

"I mean everyone of all ages. There are public high schools, and there are universities that accept women."

For a moment Rebekah closed her eyes, trying to imagine such a place. Classrooms for both boys and girls? University studies for both men and women? So many times, as she sat studying at home with Mordecai, she had wished for a university education but had never believed it was possible. She opened her eyes and looked directly into Kristin's. "Are you absolutely sure about this?" she asked.

"I'm sure."

"But in my family . . . I mean that girls help at home, then marry . . . Their fathers pick out their husbands and . . ."

Kristin crooked the little finger on her right hand, holding it out toward Rebekah. "Hold my finger with yours," she said, and when Rebekah had done so, Kristin said, "All right. Make a wish."

"A wish is nothing but a wish," Rebekah murmured.

Kristin's blue eyes burned with eagerness. "Don't *wait* for your wish to come true," she said. "You can *make* your wish come true in America."

Rebekah crooked her own little finger, hooked it with Kristin's and gave a tug. "All right, I will," she said, giggling with excitement. "I'll make it come true. In the United States Rebekah Levinsky will go to school."

CHAPTER FOUR

❖ ❖ ❖

SOFIA went below, miffed because Rebekah had insisted that she speak English. Rebekah and Kristin remained at the rail, enjoying the slow passage of the ship from the harbor channel to the sea, where it began to rise and fall rhythmically with the ocean swells. To Rebekah, who had never before seen the ocean, its vast expanse was magnificent. The gently rolling waters both excited and calmed her, and soon all other thoughts vanished from her mind.

The peace ended abruptly as a group of kitchen workers began to trundle out on deck an assortment of serving tables, eating utensils, bowls, and large kettles. Attracted by the mingled odors of steaming beef and vegetables, some of the passengers in the hold hurried up on deck, pushing and elbowing each other to get to the tables.

Rebekah stood back from the fray, watching as these travelers from all parts of a continent gathered together for a meal. Although they came from many European countries, their clothing was basically the same—dark pants, coats, and hats for the men; heavy-duty dark skirts and blouses, drab jackets, and shawls for the women, with kerchiefs covering their hair. Rebekah noticed how different each group seemed even as they were lumped together. One group waved their hands as they spoke, those in another seemed quieter, their heads closer together, nodding in emphasis. A group studied its neighbors suspiciously, and a few families reeked of olive oil and onions.

A ship's bell clanged, and the deckhands added to the shoving and shouting, as they tried to get the emigrants to form orderly lines.

The line pushed ahead, but Rebekah saw no sign of the members of her own family until Nessin's head popped into view. He gave Rebekah a wave and tried to shove forward.

It was impossible for Rebekah to reach him, so she cupped her hands around her mouth and called in Yiddish, "Where are the others?"

"Down below," he called back and gestured with his hand.

With difficulty Rebekah squeezed past those who were climbing the steep stairway and made her way to her family's bunks, where Leah sat next to Jacob. Pale and moaning, Jacob lay on his side, his head in his mother's lap.

"Jacob is seasick," Sofia announced. She plopped down on the next bunk, on which her father and grandfather were seated, shoulders slumped so their heads wouldn't bump the upper bunk.

Rebekah picked up her brother's yarmulke, which had fallen to the floor, and laid the little black skullcap back on his head. "How could Jacob be seasick already?" she asked. "The ship has gone only a short distance, and the sea is calm."

Jacob groaned loudly and put his hands over his face.

Rebekah added quickly, "Jacob will feel better on deck. The air is fresh, and the terrible smell down here is enough to make anyone feel worse. Besides"— she tried to sound cheerful—"supper is being served."

"Supper." Elias shook his head. "I took care of every detail to get to this ship but I didn't think far enough ahead. This food is not kosher. We should have brought a large supply of food with us."

Rebekah's mother rubbed her head as it bumped against the metal edge of the top bunk. "How could we have carried any more baggage? Besides, there would be no place to store all the food we'd need, and no room to prepare it."

"But we will be unable to keep kashruth. We are on this ship and therefore we cannot follow the dietary laws."

Rebekah had never in her life eaten food that was not kosher, but her little sister was too young to be concerned about the religious rules concerning eating kosher food. Sofia's lower lip began to curl into a pout. "I'm hungry," she said.

"There are times," Mordecai told Elias, "when survival means more than laws. This is one of those times. Our only choice is to adapt to the situation, and there is no reason why we cannot retain our piety. We will wash, say our prayers, and eat what we must."

"Then let us wash and go to supper." Elias calmly stood and held a hand out to Mordecai, helping him to his feet.

"I can't go with you. I'm too sick," Jacob complained loudly.

"Are you going to throw up again?" Sofia asked with interest.

"Hush!" Leah said and tapped one of Sofia's braids.

Rebekah interrupted, telling her brother, "You don't have to eat with us today, but believe me, you will feel so much better in the fresh breeze."

"You promise?"

"I promise."

Jacob allowed himself to be helped to his feet and to the men's washroom. As the family regrouped and began climbing the stairs, Mordecai asked, "Where is Nessin?"

"On deck," Rebekah said. She saw no need to get her brother into trouble for not remembering the ritual washing and prayers before meals. Maybe Nessin *had* remembered. She added, "He's waiting for us."

The bread was fresh and the food satisfied their hunger. They did not ask what they were eating. Even Jacob, who'd been seated on one end of a hatch cover and instructed by Leah to breathe deeply, began regaining color in his face.

A cool breeze riffled across the deck, and Rebekah pulled off her bandanna and loosened her hair, letting the wind lift it to tickle her cheeks and forehead.

"What are you thinking of?" Leah immediately asked Rebekah.

"Grandfather said there are times when laws must be set aside. . . ."

"On one hand we are talking about starving, and on the other hand a simple matter of forgetting all sense of propriety," she answered. "There is no reason here for you to uncover your head in public. Please tie your kerchief without any discussion."

Rebekah gave her mother a conciliatory smile and did as she had been told. She hoped the weather would remain this pleasant during their entire trip across the ocean. She planned to spend all of each day and much of each evening on deck, as far away from that ill-smelling hold as she could get.

After the meal some of the steerage passengers remained on deck, but many of them went below to clean their dishes and settle their belongings in and around their bunks. Rebekah was surprised when she noticed her mother standing alone at the railing, her eyes on the distant countryside.

As she joined her mother she saw tears running down her cheeks. "What is it, Mama? Are you ill, too?" Rebekah asked.

Leah shook her head and attempted to wipe away her tears. "There is no purpose in weeping for them," she said.

"Weeping for whom?" Rebekah put her arms around her mother.

"For those I am leaving behind."

"You mean Hava and her husband?"

"No," Leah said. "I am thinking about my parents and my children who did not live beyond their birth."

"But, Mama . . ." Rebekah couldn't finish.

Leah took Rebekah's hand and placed it against her cheek. "I know," she said softly. "None of them are living, but once they were. I was able to visit the places where they rest and remember the times when they were smiling and happy and my arms were around them. Now I am leaving them behind forever. Before, Elias came with me to say kaddish over them, but now there will be no one for them." Leah's tears were hot against Rebekah's fingers.

Rebekah silently wrapped her arms around her mother and let her cry against her shoulder until her mother straightened up and dried her face. "Of course we must be brave," Leah said as if she hadn't the right to feel her loss.

That evening, as Rebekah climbed into her bunk, she wrinkled her nose at the strong smell of garlic that permeated the dank air in the hold. Some of the steerage passengers, fearful of disease in their close quarters, had hung clusters of garlic around theirs and their children's necks to ward off germs.

Leah slapped her forehead. "How could I have forgotten to bring garlic?" she asked aloud.

"Leah," Elias said, "winter is over. How could we have known about these crowded conditions, the food or the noise? We made a decision and now let's make the best of this journey."

"What good are excuses going to be if my children get sick?" Leah fretted. "Ohhh, what kind of a mother am I?"

Rebekah said a silent prayer of thanks that her mother had forgotten the garlic and another prayer that her mother was back to her normal, worrying self. At last Rebekah tugged her blanket over her head to shut out the dim lantern light that would burn all night, and she fell asleep.

CHAPTER FIVE

✤ ✤ ✤

FOR the next three and a half days the ship followed a course that took it close to the north coast of Germany, through the English Channel, and around the south coast of England into the Irish Sea. With the exception of a few steerage passengers like Jacob, who remained ill the entire time, the emigrants settled down, adjusting to their miserable surroundings and making acquaintances of their temporary neighbors. Now and again there were angry voices raised in argument as boundaries were overstepped or one person behaved as was customary in his culture, not knowing he was offending someone from another country with different ways.

Elias and Mordecai talked with Mr. Swensen, but Leah, who never had mastered more than a few words of English, just smiled and shrugged when Mrs. Swensen tried to speak to her.

Many passengers, including Rebekah and Kristin, remained out-of-doors most of the day, and a few of the men bundled up to sleep on deck at night.

Each day Rebekah spent time with her grandfather, often walking around the main deck with him, slowing her pace to match his gait. She loved reading in English, reciting the names of cities and states in the United States, which he had been teaching her, and learning new things from him about the country that was their destination.

"I'm eager to see the Statue of Liberty in New York Bay," Mordecai confided. "The lady, who holds high a torch, welcomes all those who come to her shores."

Rebekah took a deep breath and spoke aloud the dream that had been growing in her mind. "Grandfather, Kristin told me that in the United States girls can go to school."

"School?" His eyes opened wide in amazement. "But you are fifteen, Rebekah. Schools are for the children."

Her heart beat a little faster. "There are schools for older students, and even universities. Some of them allow woman students. Kristin said so."

Mordecai shrugged, then said, "Your friend may be right, but your parents will expect you to help your mother in our new home, Rebekah. There may be schools for young women your age—who knows?—but aside from the pleasure of learning, I do not know what benefit formal schooling would be to you. You are already a young woman. Soon, your parents will arrange a good marriage for you. Your life will then be centered on your duties as a wife and mother."

Rebekah startled herself, as well as her grandfather, when she blurted, "There are other things to think about besides being a wife and mother." She looked directly at Mordecai, who had been husband, father, tradesman, student, and a fine teacher in his life. It had seemed to Rebekah, ever since she had been a small girl, that Mordecai had derived no greater pleasure from anything than from his teaching, which was not a duty but a labor of love. Rebekah felt herself blushing as she told him, "If there are woman students, then there must be woman teachers."

"This is what you would like? To be a teacher?"

"Oh, yes! I would! I really would!" Rebekah answered. To be like Mordecai, to have such knowledge and to share it, and to be admired and respected as Mordecai was for sharing his knowledge—Rebekah could imagine nothing more thrilling.

For a moment Mordecai sat and thought. Then he raised his head and smiled at Rebekah. "Who knows what will happen in the New World?" he said, more to himself than to her.

At least he didn't say my dream is impossible, Rebekah told herself.

Mordecai, with his friendliness and his command of languages, soon knew many of the travelers in steerage. He often served as translator and even peacemaker, and he continued to share nuggets of information with his family.

"Passengers in second and first class do not have to go through an examination at Ellis Island," he said on the third evening at sea. "An inspector and doctor come to the ship, and the examination amounts to only a few questions. The officials believe that those who can afford to travel in first or second class have enough money to continue to support themselves in the United States without needing public assistance."

"What *is* Ellis Island like?" Rebekah demanded.

Mordecai smiled. "Here is what I know: Ellis Island is a group of buildings large enough to hold thousands of people at one time. These buildings stand on an island in Upper New York Bay, across from Manhattan Island."

"Another island?"

"Manhattan Island is covered with very, very tall buildings. This is New York City, the place where your Uncle Avir lives with his family. It's where we all will live."

"Is New York City like the city of Hamburg? So many houses?"

"It is larger," Mordecai said, "and its buildings are taller . . . much taller . . . ten, fifteen, even twenty stories!"

Jacob interrupted by leaning over his bunk and gagging with dry heaves into the bucket his mother had appropriated and placed there.

"Rebekah!" Kristin shouted and waved from the stairway. "Come on deck! We are moving into the Liverpool harbor!"

Rebekah, her sympathy for her brother wearing thin, was glad to escape and join Kristin on deck.

Music from a string trio on the outdoor top deck fell like soft raindrops, and Rebekah lifted her face to catch every note. She could imagine the expensively dressed women in flowing gowns, dancing to the music and eating . . . well, who knew what wealthy women ate? Surely it wasn't the bland watery stews that had been served to the steerage passengers day after day.

Kristin grabbed Rebekah's hand and pulled her toward the railing. Lights sparkled along the shore, clustering ahead like a gathering of stars.

"We're coming toward the harbor," Kristin told her, "but I heard one of the ship's officers say that the passengers wouldn't board until tomorrow morning." She giggled and said, "Let's sleep outside on deck tonight, where we can see the lights and the stars."

Rebekah looked at Kristin in surprise. "Will your father let you?"

"Once he goes to sleep he snores like a steam engine and hears nothing. I can slip outside, and neither my father nor mother will notice."

Rebekah thought a moment. "Some of the men sleep outside, but I don't think any of the women do."

"One or two of the women have," Kristin said.

"How do you know?"

"Last night I sneaked outside and took a look."

Rebekah laughed, and for the first time felt bold enough to not worry about her mother's rules. "Then let's do it," she said.

"Will you have to ask your parents' permission?"

"I should," Rebekah answered.

Kristin raised an eyebrow. "If you asked, they'd say 'no.' Am I right?" Rebekah nodded. "But if you don't ask, then they cannot later say they have forbidden it!"

Rebekah lowered her voice. "I suppose that's so," she said slowly. But she couldn't help grinning a little at Kristin's clever logic.

What is happening to me? Rebekah wondered. *I have always been an obedient and dutiful daughter, yet I'm thinking and saying and doing things I never would have thought of back home.*

CHAPTER SIX

❖ ❖ ❖

IT wasn't just Kristin's father who snored loudly. Snores came from every direction, reverberating throughout the hold, so between the noise and her nervousness over being caught Rebekah had no trouble staying awake until it was time to join Kristin on the upper deck.

Rebekah had waited her turn at the privy for women, trying to hold her breath while she was in the cramped, dirty, foul-smelling space. There were faucets of cold salt water along the outer wall of the room for washing, but the basins they emptied into were dirty. In one basin a woman was soaking soiled clothing. Another basin was crusted with dried vomit that had not been washed out. Rebekah tried to find the cleanest basin possible, then hurriedly rinsed her hands and face, her eyes stinging from the cold salt water.

Now she lay on her bunk, her jacket wrapped tightly around her as usual, until she heard Kristin's whispered signal. Smothering their giggles, the girls tied their kerchiefs, tugged on their boots, and dropped quietly to the floor, taking their shawls and blankets with them. With the few ship's lanterns to light the way, Kristin ran toward the stairway; but Rebekah stopped to look back and saw her brother Jacob watching her with mournful eyes. She dropped to her knees and put her lips close to his ear. "Come with us," she said. "We're going to sleep outside."

Wearily, he shook his head, but Rebekah took a firm grip on his arm. "Come," she said, tugging at her brother. "The ship isn't moving, and the fresh night air will help you feel better." She fumbled for his coat, which had been folded and laid over the end of his bunk. "And don't make any noise!" she whispered.

Jacob, too weak and ill to disobey, did as Rebekah told him, and crawled from his bed. He straightened the tangled tassels of his tsitsith, which hung below his waist both front and back, bundled into his coat and scarf, and Rebekah pushed him ahead up the stairway and through the open hatch.

Kristin's mouth opened with surprise as she saw Jacob, but before she had a chance to say anything, Rebekah stated, "Jacob needs to get away from that horrible stench." And to her brother she said, "Now breathe deeply. Again . . . again."

"I've found us a place," Kristin said, but she glanced dubiously at Jacob before she led them forward to where a few other people had settled down on one of the closed hatch covers. Some of them smiled and nodded as Rebekah, Kristin, and Jacob joined them.

A man asked them something, but the three of them didn't understand his language, so they shrugged and shook their heads.

"We're from Russia," Jacob said in Yiddish.

At the same time, Rebekah said in Russian, "Does anyone here speak Russian?"

And Kristin said in Swedish, repeating herself in English, "I'm from Sweden."

A few people nodded recognition, and some shrugged and settled against each other, trying to find comfortable positions; but a tall, slender, dark-haired boy, who was probably only a year or two older than Rebekah, left the group. He waited until Rebekah had seated herself, then sat down next to her. Rebekah tried to squeeze over, closer to Kristin, but there was only so much room, and the three of them were wedged together.

"Good evening," the boy said in Yiddish.

Rebekah tilted her head toward Kristin as she asked in his language, "Can you speak English?"

"Very little," he answered.

"I don't want to speak another language in front of my friend," Rebekah told him.

"Very well . . . Rebekah," he said in English.

Startled, she asked, "How do you know my name?"

The boy suddenly grinned and reached into the inside pocket of his jacket, pulling out a wooden flute. Without answering he put the mouthpiece of the flute to his lips. Soft notes tumbled out in a trill, followed by a softer, slower tune that slowly wrapped around Rebekah's shoulders like her woolen shawl, comforting and warm.

Around them voices murmured, then hushed, as the music cast its spell. Jacob sighed with pleasure and stretched out on the deck at Rebekah's feet. With a smile on his face he placed his head on his hands and closed his eyes, and his breathing deepened. It was the first comfortable sleep that poor, seasick Jacob had enjoyed since the Levinskys had boarded the ship.

The boy continued playing, his music as coaxing as a smile, as gentle as a kiss. Kristin lay her head on Rebekah's shoulder, and soon it was heavy with sleep.

Rebekah found it hard to keep her eyes open. She began to dream that the music floated away into the night, joining the stars in a melody that faded to a whisper and vanished into the heavens. In her dream her head rested against someone's chest. His arm was snug around her shoulders, and his lips softly brushed her forehead.

The gray light of early dawn awoke Rebekah, and she sat up, confused, as she looked at the empty place next to her. Where was the boy with the flute? The one who knew her name but hadn't told her his own? Blushing, she vividly remembered her dream. It had been just a dream, hadn't it?

Kristin awoke and stretched, yawning widely. When she fully opened her eyes she looked around and asked, "Where is he?"

"Who?" Rebekah whispered.

"That boy with the flute. When did he leave?"

"I don't know," Rebekah said. She could still feel his arm around her shoulders and his lips against her forehead. It hadn't been a dream. It had been real. Kristin was rubbing sleep from her eyes, and Rebekah was thankful that her friend couldn't see the blush that reddened her cheeks.

Around the girls people were stirring as daylight awakened them. It was going to be another sunny day, cool and beautiful.

"Let's sleep outside again," Kristin said, "and maybe the boy with the flute will come back. He was good-looking, wasn't he!" Kristin laughed knowingly, and Rebekah realized that Kristin hadn't missed a thing.

Suddenly there was the sound of shoes clattering rapidly along the deck, and Rebekah's mother came into view. Leah stopped short, one hand pressed against her heart, when she saw Rebekah and Jacob.

Oy vey, Rebekah thought.

"When I woke up and saw that you and Jacob were gone, my heart went into my throat!" Leah began. "We are in port. You could have been abducted from the ship. You were sleeping out here all night, weren't you?" She pointed at Jacob. "Look at the poor boy—sleeping on the hard deck!"

"Mama," Rebekah interrupted. "It is just as you said. Jacob is *sleeping.*"

"What?"

"He's sleeping, and he has slept all night long. It's the first time he's been able to sleep since we boarded the ship."

Jacob, his slumber disturbed by the familiar voices, awoke and struggled to a sitting position. He stretched and arched his back and smiled up at Leah. "Mama!" he said. "Rebekah told me that I'd be able to sleep if I came outside, and she was right."

Leah bent to hold Jacob's face, tilting it up to examine it as though she had never seen it before. "There's color in your cheeks," she said with amazement.

"I'm hungry," Jacob said. "Is it time yet for food?"

As Leah stepped back and beamed, Kristin said in English, "Good morning, Mrs. Levinsky."

"Good morning, Kristin," Leah answered slowly and precisely in English.

Kristin hopped up, folding her blanket and tugging her shawl around her shoulders. "I'd better go below before my parents miss me," she said, and raced toward the open hatchway.

Leah's eyes narrowed as she studied the faces of those passengers who were on deck. "They are mostly men," she said in shock.

Rebekah studied the faces, too, looking for the boy with the flute, but he was nowhere in sight. "Some of the women slept outside also," she insisted. "Look, there are two of them."

"But not as many women as there were men."

"Mama, it's all right."

"Oh? Where is it written that it's all right for a young girl to sleep outside, away from her family, in the company of strange men?"

Jacob got to his feet and put an arm around his mother's shoulders. "Don't scold Rebekah, Mama," he said. "I was with her."

"It still isn't a proper thing to do."

"Mama, think about it. Rebekah helped me sleep. For the first time since we left Hamburg I was able to sleep. You should be thanking her."

Leah's eyebrows rose in surprise, but she reached for Rebekah's hand. "Thank you for helping Jacob, Rebekah. But this sleeping outside on deck is something we will have to discuss with your father."

"I'll be glad to talk to Papa," Jacob said. "That hold smells like a garbage dump. No, even worse!"

"Well ...," Leah said with uncertainty, and Rebekah hoped the matter would end there. She never would be allowed to come on deck again to sleep if it weren't for Jacob's help. Jacob was a boy—almost a man—and his opinions were considered with respect, whereas Rebekah, being a girl . . . She sighed but thought again with wonder about what Kristin had told her of America.

Leah looked across the dock toward the city of Liverpool. "We have relatives in England," she said.

"I've never heard about them. Who?" Rebekah asked.

"Cousins of Mordecai's. They left our village many years before you were born. There are two of them—brothers."

"Will we meet these cousins?"

"No," Leah said. "There is not enough time. They live in London, much too far away."

She turned toward the open hatch, but Rebekah continued to gaze toward the land. Relatives in England, relatives in America . . . Her close family life in the shtetl was rapidly enlarging.

Breakfast was a combination of dried herring and potatoes. Rebekah was hungry enough to wolf down the food. She sat on deck with her father, her empty plate on her lap, her tin cup of coffee cradled in both hands, and questioned him about their lives-to-be in the United States. But Elias, who had eaten very little of his meal, gave only noncommittal answers.

Rebekah tried to hide her impatience. "Papa," she finally said, "don't you know where we will live? Don't you know what we'll be doing?"

As he turned toward her, she could see the misery

in his eyes, and she wished she had kept her questions to herself.

"No, Rebekah, I don't know," Elias said, his voice as firm and controlled as ever. "I have always led a simple life. I have worked hard as a tailor and taken pride in my work. On some occasions times have been very difficult, but I have always managed to provide for my family. Yet, here I am fleeing the czar's soldiers by taking my wife and children to a country that is strange to me. We'll live in a very large city, and I do not know yet how I will care for all of you."

"But Uncle Avir said he would have a job for you, Papa, and tailors should have much more work in a city than in our shtetl . . . shouldn't they?"

"I can only hope," he answered.

Leah stepped up, putting a hand on her husband's shoulder. "Life in the United States will be good for all of us," she said firmly. She turned her gaze on Rebekah. "Don't expect instant answers to all your questions, daughter. Life is a series of questions, and you'll have to find your own answers for most of them."

"I'm sorry," Rebekah began, but her mother interrupted with a smile and a quick shake of her head.

"There is no need to be sorry. Here . . . as soon as your father has finished eating you can help by taking the dishes down to be washed."

Elias quickly finished his meal and handed his dishes to Rebekah.

Rebekah took care of her chores quickly. During the rest of the morning she looked for the boy with the flute but was unable to see him in the horde of steerage passengers who crowded the deck. After the noon meal her attention was diverted by the new people who had begun boarding the ship.

She and Kristin squeezed in among the others who were leaning on the rail of the main deck to watch stylishly dressed women walk up the gangplanks, escorted by their equally stylish male companions.

Rebekah nodded toward a woman in a narrow-waisted blue coat with silver buttons. "I would like to have a coat like that. Wearing it would make me feel beautiful."

"You are beautiful," a voice said, and Rebekah whirled to see the boy with the flute.

Rebekah quickly stared down at her shoes, unable to meet his eyes. "I am terribly embarrassed about last night," she said. "Your music was lovely, and it soothed away our problems. It helped us all to fall asleep. And that's where I . . ." She began again. "As I slept, if I accidentally happened to rest my head on your shoulder I apologize, because . . ."

She forced herself to draw on her courage and decided to face him, but when she looked again he was gone. Frantically, she scanned the crowd, but he was nowhere in sight.

CHAPTER SEVEN

✤ ✤ ✤

SCRAMBLING back to Kristin's side, Rebekah stammered, "Kristin! I saw the boy with the flute, and he talked to me again, but he disappeared."

"He'll be back," Kristin said, her attention turned to something interesting. "Here come the steerage passengers."

Rebekah watched the people who were being herded in a cluster along the dock toward the gangplank that led to the main deck. Most of the emigrants were young men, and there were only two families with children.

"How can they fit any more people down in the hold?" Rebekah murmured.

Behind a rope that a dockhand had stretched across the pier to keep out nonpassengers stood a woman with two little girls. One of the children seemed to be about Sofia's age, the other only three or four years old. Both girls were sobbing. "Rosie! Don't go! Rosie, don't leave us!" The youngest screamed loudly, over and over.

In the midst of the group of emigrants, a tall girl in a faded dress and shawl, her bright red hair hanging free from under a skimpy kerchief, was crying heartbrokenly. Occasionally, as the line moved, she turned and waved to the little ones, trying to muster a smile, but the man with her gripped her arm and pulled her along with the crowd, which surged forward as the gangplank was opened to them.

Rebekah noticed that the girl the children had called Rosie looked as if she were close to her own age. Rosie certainly was not old enough to be the children's mother. Rebekah thought what it would be like to be leaving Sofia. Her vision blurred, and she quickly wiped her eyes with the back of one hand.

The small band of emigrants disappeared into the hold, the human barricades moved away, and some of the passengers drifted back from the railing.

In German Rebekah asked one of the deckhands who was passing by, "When will the ship leave?"

"Very early tomorrow morning," he answered with a smile. "Two weeks, and you will be in the United States."

Rebekah turned to Kristin. "Two weeks!" she cried in English, and her heart began to beat faster.

"There'll be partying on deck tonight," the sailor added. "There often is the last night before sailing."

"A party? Who's having a party?"

"You'll see," he answered, and strode on down the deck.

Someone brushed against Rebekah, and she jumped out of the way only to turn and see the red-haired girl. Rosie was at the rail, her hand half-raised in a wave as she leaned over, staring across the pier into the distance. A strangled sob escaped her, and she slumped, her shoulders trembling as she began to cry.

Rebekah looked at the rope, which was still stretched across the deck, and saw that the woman and two children had gone. Impulsively, she put a hand on the girl's shoulder. "I'm so sorry, Rosie," she said.

The girl jerked with surprise, but she managed with great effort to gain control of her feelings. She mopped at her reddened, swollen eyes with an already soggy handkerchief. "How do you know my name?"

"I overheard your sisters crying," Rebekah replied.

"I'd hoped to get a last look at my mother and my sisters," Rosie said in an accent Rebekah had never heard before. "They came over with us on a friend's fishing boat, and now, they're on their way back to Drogheda. I'll see them in two years, the good Lord willing." She gave a last shuddering, dry sob and added, "Ma said it's pure foolishness to waste time with tears."

"Foolish or not, sometimes you can't help crying," Rebekah said. "My family is with me, but I still cried at leaving my home and my friends. Even the adults sometimes cry," she said, remembering her mother's sadness.

"I cried buckets and buckets of tears when I had to leave my grandmother," Kristin volunteered. "I wanted so badly to stay in Sweden."

"So, we are all in this together." The girl sighed and brushed a strand of gleaming red hair back from her cheek. "My full name is Rose Carney," she said.

"I'm Rebekah Levinsky."

"And I'm Kristin Swensen." Kristin motioned

49

toward a vacant spot on one of the hatch covers. "Let's all sit down," she said to Rose. "Rebekah and I stay out of that awful hold as much as possible. Your father can take care of putting your things away for you."

"That's my uncle Jimmy, not my father," Rose said as she perched between Rebekah and Kristin. "Jimmy had to travel with me, because my father can't come from Chicago to meet me at Ellis Island. My father went to live in the United States four years ago, before my little sister Meggie was born. He sent home money to bring over my two older brothers, one at a time. Now it's my turn to go. With all of us working hard and saving our money, soon Ma, Bridget, and Meggie will be able to come over together. Then we'll be a family again."

"What do you mean, your uncle had to travel with you?" Kristin asked.

"Uncle Jimmy has wanted to go to the United States for a long time, so I was his excuse. You see, the people at Ellis Island have a rule that any female traveling alone has to be met by a male member of her family. If my father planned to meet me and he was late, they'd keep me there until he showed up, but only for two weeks. If he didn't show up by then, they'd send me back."

"Like a spoiled fish!" Kristin said indignantly.

Rose smiled. "Since I'm not a spoiled fish, it's easier to have my Uncle Jimmy come along. He'll escort me on the train to Chicago." She paused and looked thoughtful. "Do you know, I had just reached my twelfth birthday when my father left Ireland, and sometimes I have a hard time remembering what he looks like."

Rebekah, who thought how much she would hate having her family separated, didn't know what to say, so she was relieved when Kristin changed the subject. "We were told there's going to be a party tonight."

"A party? What kind of party?"

"We don't know."

"In a group this size, there should be many musicians," Rose answered, and her eyes shone. "If there'll be music, then it follows there'll be dancing."

Kristin frowned. "Our pastor was very strict. He didn't approve of social dancing."

Rose looked surprised and said, "There never was a stricter man than our pastor, Father O'Brien, but not a word has he ever said against dancing. It's a wholesome enough way to enjoy an evening."

"Pastor Larsen says it's a tool of the devil." Kristin turned to Rebekah. "Do you dance, Rebekah?"

"Oh, no!" Rebekah said. "At least not in public. We had music for special occasions, like weddings, but the men danced together, and some of the women danced with each other behind a partition."

Rose's eyes widened. "The men and women didn't dance with each other?"

"You mean they do in Ireland?"

"Of course," she said.

Rebekah was shocked. She had never heard of men and women dancing together and could imagine what her mother would say about such scandalous behavior. But Kristin looked impressed as she asked, "Rose, do you dance?"

Rose smiled and her eyes sparkled. "I love to dance—especially a jig."

Kristin beamed at Rose with a wicked gleam in

her eyes. "I've never seen anyone dance a jig," she said. "This is going to be a very interesting party."

Although no one actually planned a party, there was a strange spirit that crackled through the ship, an electric excitement overriding exhaustion, worry, and fear. A few of the women had exchanged their drab kerchiefs and dresses for festive ones, and children's faces had been scrubbed. There was music, and there was dancing; and when Rose's Uncle Jimmy jumped to the top of one of the hatches with a fiddle, he called to his niece to perform.

It was a strange kind of dance, Rebekah thought. Rose's feet flashed in a pattern of steps so intricate that some of the watchers murmured in appreciation, but she kept her shoulders and upper body rigid, and her hands remained at her sides. Rebekah, who would have been mortified to be the center of attention, was astonished to see the smile on Rose's lips and the sparkle in her eyes. Rebekah wondered what her mother was thinking, but realized she almost didn't care.

When the entertainment ended, Rebekah, Kristin, and Rose collected their shawls and blankets and found a place to sleep on deck along with Jacob. Jacob was asleep in a moment; Kristin and Rose stirred around like kittens arranging their nest, then settled down and soon followed.

Rebekah remained awake. With a pang she realized that she was watching and waiting for the boy with the flute. She was hoping he'd return with his haunting music and, as scandalous as she knew it was, his arm around her. Rebekah wondered how she could feel so different in just a short time. She'd never had any adventure in her life, and now it was making her feel so many new things.

Sleep finally crept over Rebekah, and she dreamed that near her a soft flute was playing. The notes were low and soothing, brushing her cheek and tickling her earlobe.

Early in the morning, when the eastern sky had barely lightened to gray, Rebekah was jolted from sleep as deckhands began to make the ship ready for departure. "You'll all have to move," one of them ordered, and the steerage passengers scrambled to their feet, pulling their shawls and blankets more tightly around their necks and shoulders as they made their way to the open hatch.

"The air's cold enough to wake the dead," Rose complained.

"But you slept well, didn't you?" Kristin asked.

"Better than I would have down below," Rose answered, then stopped, frowning as she thought. "Did I hear someone playing a flute during the night?"

Rebekah started, but one corner of Kristin's mouth twitched into a mischievous smile, and she said, "I woke just enough to see him sitting with his back against the funnel. He was playing his flute, never for a moment taking his eyes off our own Rebekah's face."

Rebekah blushed a hot red as Rose looked at her. "Who is Kristin talking about?" Rose asked.

"I don't know," Rebekah answered. "He's a boy who plays his flute, then disappears. He's never told us his name."

Where had he come from? And why was he being so mysterious? It would not be proper for a young woman to ask a stranger his name, but being proper seemed less and less important in changing times like these.

CHAPTER EIGHT

❖ ❖ ❖

In the morning, Rebekah's parents did not complain. They seemed satisfied that Jacob was sleeping again and that he was with Rebekah through the night.

For breakfast, the steerage passengers were fed chunks of bread and a lumpy, hot gruel. Even before they ate they were urged to hurry.

No one had to urge Rebekah. She was eager for the ship to put out to sea.

She had cleaned her dishes and was halfway up the stairs to the main deck when a blast of the ship's horn shuddered throughout the ship. She scrambled and tripped as the large screws under the hold turned with a great creaking and thumping, and the ship rocked as it was pushed away from the pier. On deck, Rebekah staggered to grip the railing. She watched the dock recede into the distance, then lifted her face to catch the cold salt breeze and to watch the seagulls cry and swoop as they followed the ship, hoping for food.

"Good morning, Rebekah." A voice spoke in Yiddish close to her right ear, and Rebekah turned sharply, looking up into the face of the mysterious boy.

"Oh!" was all she could think of to reply.

He waited for her to speak, then shrugged and turned as if he were leaving.

No! He couldn't! Rebekah wanted to know so much about him. She reached out and clasped his wrist. "Please don't leave," she said. "I . . . I want to thank you for your beautiful music."

He smiled and somehow slid her hand down from his wrist so that his fingers were firmly entwined with her own. Holding hands in public! Rebekah never would have dreamed of doing such a thing back home, but she left her hand in his and felt the warmth of his fingers spread up her arm and into her face.

"You and your family come from a town not far from mine," he told her.

Rebekah was puzzled. "How do you know me?"

"I noticed you with your family and your friends. You have a wonderful smile, Rebekah. It shines in your eyes and makes everyone around you want to smile, too. I asked your brother Nessin to tell me your name. I also know that you are two and a half years younger than I am and that you and your family are going to live in New York City, as I am when I join my father and four older brothers."

Rebekah smiled self-consciously, embarrassed by his praise. "I don't know your name."

He hesitated, then said, "Aaron. Aaron Mirsch."

Aaron was a strong name, and he was obviously a nice person. *Very* nice. In spite of the chill air, Rebekah's hand—the one Aaron was still holding—began to perspire.

"Why didn't you tell me your name before this?" Rebekah asked. "Why were you so . . . mysterious?"

"I . . . For a while I believed there were reasons we'd never meet again, but things are different in the United States, so I told myself that maybe . . ."

"What reasons?"

"I'll tell you someday," he said and leaned on the rail, watching the progress of the ship.

As the tugs backed the ship far from land and turned it to face the open sea, many of the passengers began to come up on deck.

Rebekah heard her mother calling her from across the deck, and she quickly pulled her hand from Aaron's as she twisted around, searching the crowd that was pressing toward the rail. "Here I am, Mama!" Rebekah called.

"I'd like you to meet my mother," she said to Aaron, but he had disappeared. Rebekah stared at her hand, still warm and pink from having been held, as though Aaron were somehow hiding within her palm.

Leah elbowed toward Rebekah, pushing Sofia ahead of her all the way. They reminded Rebekah of the steamship and one of its little tugs in reverse positions, and she laughed.

Leah was in no mood for laughter. "Already Jacob is seasick again," she said.

"I'll help you, Mama," Rebekah told her and took a step toward her, but her mother impatiently waved her back.

"That's not the help I need right now," she announced as she thrust her youngest daughter forward. "Just keep an eye on Sofia." Head down, Leah created a return path through the crowd.

"That ocean looks just like the other one," Sofia said as she perched on tiptoe, her nose against the rail.

"It's the same ocean we were on when we arrived in Liverpool," Rebekah told her. "It's called the Irish Sea."

"When do we get to the real ocean—the big one?"

"Very soon," Rebekah promised. "By tomorrow you'll be able to look all around and not see any land at all."

The tugs backed away from the ship, and it changed direction, moving forward. The sea was choppy, and as the prow dipped, waves splashed against it, shooting sprays of icy water high into the air. Rebekah smiled as a droplet stung her cheek.

"This is fun," Sofia said. She smiled up at her sister. "Will it be like this all the way to the United States?"

"As long as we have good weather," Rebekah said.

"Then I'm glad now that we're going to the United States."

Rebekah looked at Sofia. "Weren't you always glad?"

"No," she said, "because Mama cried, and sometimes you cried, and I didn't want to leave our warm feather bed."

"I'm sorry, Sofia," Rebekah said, suddenly repentant for having thought only of her own unhappiness at leaving and not of how her little sister might feel.

"When we get to the United States, will we have our own house? And will we have a feather bed to share again?"

Rebekah bent to hug Sofia. "Uncle Avir promised

Papa he would find us a new home, and I know that Mama will make sure we have a very comfortable bed."

The ship lurched against a high wave, and spray shot over the crowd. Some ran for cover, and others followed them into the hold, but Rebekah and Sofia stayed at the rail, bracing their feet against the pitching of the ship and laughing at the spray.

Someone thudded against the railing, rudely jostling Rebekah, and she turned indignantly to see Nessin laughing at her. "Do you like this up and down and up and down?" he asked. "Or are you going to be like Jacob and get all green-faced and sick?" He pretended to gag, making a horrible retching sound.

"You're sickening, Nessin!" Sofia shouted, but she broke into giggles.

Rebekah ignored Nessin's attempt at humor and asked, "So tell me, who is Aaron Mirsch?"

Nessin's grin faded. "Don't be mad, Rebekah. You don't need to tell . . . anybody . . . about it."

Anybody meant their parents. "Why shouldn't I tell them?" she demanded. "What are you talking about?"

Nessin shrugged. "Don't get all excited. It was just a prank. Aaron Mirsch asked me about you, and I answered his questions. I thought it was funny."

"Why should it be funny?"

He threw a quick glance at her from the corners of his eyes. "Because a boy shouldn't ask about a girl, you know that. He doesn't have a chance with you, that's why, too. He knows it. All his questions about you and his wanting to meet you are useless."

Nessin shifted uncomfortably and turned to leave, but Rebekah caught his arm.

Nessin sighed. "Look, Rebekah," he said. "In the first place, you've got a couple of years before a marriage is arranged for you, and when it is it won't be with him. Parents look for someone from a family with a good background, especially our parents."

"Like a rabbi's son," she said with a trace of bitterness. One of her friends—two years older—had been wed to the son of a rabbi. The young man was so unpleasant and mean-spirited that Rebekah knew her friend was miserable now.

Nessin caught her tone of voice, but simply agreed enthusiastically. "That's what every parent hopes for," he said, "although they'd accept the son of a successful merchant." He paused and looked thoughtful. "Say! Having a brother for a rabbi might be in my favor. When Jacob finishes his studies and becomes a rabbi, then maybe I'll start to look around for a wife."

Another sheet of spray slapped the deck, and Sofia jumped and screeched with delight.

"You didn't finish telling me about Aaron," Rebekah said.

"I know a fellow who knows his family," Nessin said. "The Mirsch family was very poor, but somehow his father and older brothers left for America. A few months ago Aaron's mother died, so now he is going to join his father." Nessin paused and added quietly, "I have heard a rumor that the Mirschs don't observe kashruth or keep Shabbas now that the mother is dead."

So that's why Aaron had been so mysterious about

himself. What Nessin was saying was very serious, and Rebekah shuddered.

Nessin, whose shoulder was pressed against Rebekah's, felt her reaction and looked at her with surprise. "What is this?" he asked. "Surely, you weren't thinking that . . ."

"What chutzpah!" Rebekah snapped in anger. "You are a *yold* if you think I'm looking for a husband!"

Nessin chuckled, not the least bit bothered by her insults. "Then there's no problem," he said. He turned from the rail, adding, "I'm going to walk up near the prow."

"You'll get drenched."

"Want to come with me?"

"No!" Rebekah shouted after him.

Sofia hung on to the rail, intent on watching the whitecaps on the water, squealing each time the breeze splattered them with cold spray, so Rebekah had time to think. As she had told Nessin, she was not in the market for a husband—certainly not at the age of fifteen—so why did she suddenly have such a heavy lump of disappointment in the pit of her stomach?

Was it because a boy could be looked down on for what other members of his family did, even though he had no responsibility for their actions? Would his friendship, his kindness, his tender smile, and his beautiful music count for nothing with any respectable Orthodox family because his family didn't obey Orthodox Jewish law?

Rebekah let out a long sigh, but an idea suddenly sparked in her mind with such brightness that her discouragement disappeared. Everything in the United

States seemed to be different from the way it was in Russia. Very well, then, maybe Aaron's position would be different, too. Mordecai had told Rebekah that the United States was a country of self-made men who valued independence, so maybe whatever Aaron made of himself would be all that was considered.

Maybe . . . in the United States even the way marriages were arranged would be different. Maybe . . . a woman could *choose* the man she wanted to marry. Maybe she wouldn't have to get married at all if she didn't want to! Rebekah choked back a laugh.

Sofia looked up. "Rebekah?" she asked. "Are you all right?"

"I'm fine," Rebekah answered. "I just realized that all of a sudden *I'm* actually looking forward to arriving in the United States, too."

CHAPTER NINE

✤ ✤ ✤

I T was not until evening that the sea calmed and the voyage became more smooth. Rebekah, Kristin, and Rose, congratulating themselves for not getting seasick, had lots of time to chat about the lives they had left behind and to speculate about what their lives would be like once they reached the United States.

"My Uncle Avir told Father it is easy for a man to make money if he is willing to work hard," Rebekah told them.

"My father said the people who make money have to know the right people," Rose said.

"My father says a man can grow wealthy if he owns enough land," Kristin added.

The three girls automatically looked up to the top deck.

"I wonder what it would be like to be wealthy and travel only in first class," Rose murmured.

A voice broke in, and Rebekah turned to see Rose's Uncle Jimmy grinning at them. "You'd have your own stateroom with electric lights instead of lanterns," he said, "and jewels and silk gowns to wear, and far better food than we've been getting in steerage."

He swept his hat before them in a deep bow, plopped it jauntily on his head, and left, still grinning.

"Your uncle's in good humor," Kristin said to Rose.

"He always is," Rose said, "even when you'd rather he'd just calm down a bit."

Rebekah glanced at some newly washed clothes that had been hung out to dry on lines strung near the stern. "If we were wealthy, there'd be someone to do our laundry for us," she said.

Kristin decide to make it a game. "We'd wear big hats to keep off the sun and sit in those lounge chairs we saw on the top deck."

"And do nothing all day long," Rebekah said. She began to laugh. "I'd hate having nothing to do. Wouldn't that be boring?"

"It would be better than milking cows at five o'clock in the morning," Kristin answered.

"You'd have lots of other wealthy people around you so you could all do nothing together," Rose said.

As the three girls laughed, Rebekah thought how glad she was that Kristin and Rose were on the ship, too. The two weeks at sea wouldn't seem nearly as long as it would have without them.

For the next three days many of the passengers enjoyed being out in the fresh air, so the main deck was crowded. Rebekah took turns with her mother in caring for Jacob, and valued the time she was free to enjoy the brisk air on deck.

Rose was almost always free to do as she pleased,

and Kristin seemed to want to spend as much time as possible away from her parents, so the three girls were often together. But during the times when Kristin and Rose were not at hand, Aaron would suddenly appear, and Rebekah began to feel at ease with him, happy in his company.

"What will you do when you reach the United States?" she asked him.

Aaron picked up his flute and studied it. "My father works in a clothing factory. I'll have a job there, too."

"What about your music?"

"I'm not a trained musician. My flute is only for my own pleasure."

"And mine." He looked so pleased that Rebekah smiled and added, "Maybe in the United States you can study music. Russian music is so beautiful. Maybe in the new country people will want to hear it."

"It takes money for lessons, and factory jobs don't pay that well."

Rebekah thought about the education she wanted so desperately. "I believe," she said slowly, each word a promise to herself, "that if you truly want something and you're willing to work for it, then nothing can stop you from getting it."

"How about a father who wants only your paycheck?"

Rebekah turned and urgently grasped the rough fabric of Aaron's coat in both fists. "There's freedom and opportunity in the United States! If you love your music, then you should fight for it! You can't give up! I won't let you!"

Aaron clasped Rebekah's hands and held them

firmly as he studied her with an expression both joyful and solemn. "Do you care that much about me, Rebekah?" he asked.

"You're my friend. I care about all my friends."

"Is that all I am—a friend?"

"Aaron," Rebekah answered firmly, "I am only fifteen. I am too young to even think of . . . of anything beyond friendship." The look in his eyes told her this wasn't answer enough. She recited the words she had so often heard: "When my parents decide that I've reached the proper age, they'll find a suitable husband for me."

Aaron let go of Rebekah's hands and sighed. "You tell me to work for what I want, but you are willing to have other people plan your life for you. Doesn't the new country hold any freedom and opportunity for you?"

When she didn't answer immediately, Aaron stepped back and strode across the deck to the open hatchway leading to the hold.

Rebekah's mind churned, and she clamped her hands on each side of her head, as though she could hold her thoughts in place. There must be freedom and opportunity for everyone who came to the United States, but she would have to see it for herself. Didn't men receive a larger share of it than women? Hadn't this always been the way of the world? Could the United States really be any different?

On the fourth day out of Liverpool the wind blew hard enough to stir up good-sized waves, slamming them against the ship, and it began to rain. Within minutes the rain beat down in torrents, and the wind howled and shrieked louder and more persistently than the ship's rasping horn.

Those passengers still above the hold rushed toward the open hatchway, slipping and sliding on the slick decks. A few stragglers followed them only when sailors ordered them down into the hold for safety's sake.

Rebekah was one of the stragglers. She had been in the hold earlier to sit with Jacob, and when Leah had come to take her place, Rebekah had rushed out of the foul stench of the place, gulping in the cold, wet air.

Halfway down the stairs she looked back and saw four sailors lift the hatch cover, struggling against the wind.

"What are you doing?" Rebekah screamed at them.

"We have to bolt this down," one of the sailors said.

"You can't! The smell! The . . ."

"We have to, for your own safety," he yelled back, and the hatch cover fell into place.

Rebekah could hear the bolts being fastened, and she shivered. All the steerage passengers had been crammed into the hold and were locked in. They couldn't get out! Even if the ship were to sink!

The ship rolled violently, throwing Rebekah off balance, and she skidded on the slippery stairway, bouncing down a couple of steps until she stopped herself by catching the handrail and clinging to it. Her legs were so wobbly she couldn't stand, and she broke into a sweat as she thought of being trapped in the hold. The lanterns swung wildly, casting crazy, leaping shadows, and here and there Rebekah could hear the sound of retching and vomiting.

Bile rose in her throat, and she clapped a hand over her mouth, forcing it down. The stink in this place was enough to make anyone ill, and the irregular pitching of the ship added to the horror.

Enough! She was wasting time. Her family might need her.

Rebekah had no sooner reached her family's bunks than the ship seemed to rise in the air, stagger, then slam to the water with a crash. Sharp cries and shrieks of terror echoed throughout the hold. To keep from falling, Rebekah clung to the post that supported the upper bunk, and as the ship steadied itself, she found a sure hold.

Her mother had tumbled to the floor and was sitting spraddle-legged, her face white with fear. Jacob moaned, Sofia began a high-pitched wail, and Nessin, who clung to one of the top bunks, stared at Rebekah with frightened eyes.

"Mama, are you hurt?" Rebekah asked as she held out a hand to help her mother up.

"The ship is sinking," Leah whispered.

"No, it isn't," Rebekah answered. *Not yet.* She cast an eye toward Elias and Mordecai, who were huddled on one bottom bunk. Draped in their prayer shawls, siddurs held close to their faces, they read the prayers aloud.

Rebekah struggled to keep her balance as the ship rocked. "Mama, sit here—at the end of the bunk," she ordered. "Hold on tightly."

"Jacob . . ."

"Jacob will be all right where he is."

"Sofia?"

"Here she is." Rebekah snatched her little sister up from the bunk where she'd been cowering and thrust her under her mother's arm. Mother and daughter clung to each other.

Up rose the ship again, to the sound of screams and shouted prayers, and Rebekah hugged the bunk support tightly, squeezing her eyes shut as the ship dropped with a crash against the churning water.

As the ship steadied itself and rolled, Rebekah opened her eyes and found herself looking directly into Kristin's.

"I'll never do another wicked thing as long as I live!" Kristin moaned.

"There's water in the hold!" someone screamed. "The ship is sinking!"

"No, it's *not*!" Rebekah shouted. "It's not, it's not, it's not!"

The hatch cover was suddenly removed, and a group of sailors wrapped in huge, black, oiled rain-coats flapped down into the hold like giant bats. While some of them turned on the bilge pumps, others set up a bucket chain and drained the water that had seeped in and spread over one end of the hold.

They worked quickly and efficiently, then were gone, the hatch cover bolted back into place. The storm continued, and the ship raised high and slammed down, raised and slammed, over and over and over again.

A man staggered halfway up the steps and beat with his fists against the hatch cover. "Let me out!" he shouted. "I want to jump into the sea! I want to die! I can't stand this any longer!"

But the ship lurched, throwing him off balance, and he rolled down the steps, vomiting where he lay.

"We're all going to die!" someone cried.

"No, we're not," Rebekah insisted. She shut out the wails and cries and retching noises that filled the hold, wondering to herself why she was so positive they would all survive.

She thought about her conversation about freedom and independence with Aaron. She knew now what they meant in her life. She was going to the United States. She was going to go to school. She—Rebekah—was going to have an education and make something of herself. Nothing was going to get in her way.

As the storm went on, Rebekah lost track of time. She knew only that days were passing. Once when there seemed to be a lull in the noise and movement of the ship, she was sure that the worst was over, but it started again. She curled into one of the bottom bunks, dozing until she was awakened by the rolling ship flipping her to the floor.

Finally, gradually, the heaving of the big ship grew less and less powerful, until it settled into a steady roll. Rebekah awoke from sleep to hear people talking instead of moaning. Passengers began climbing from their bunks with surprised expressions on their faces, stretching and studying their arms and legs, as though making sure they were still in place.

The hatch cover was removed, and fresh air and golden afternoon sunlight streamed through. Deckhands came down with rags and buckets, handing them out to the steerage passengers, so they could clean up the mess that covered the floor. The vile-smelling contents of bucket after bucket were emptied overboard, and the deck was swept down.

When all was in order again, and clothes and bedding had been laid outside to air and dry, the hungry passengers ate. After the meal, Rebekah found Aaron by following the gentle sound of his flute. He sat behind one of the funnels, and although the deck was cold and still a little damp, Rebekah sat down next to him.

He looked at her and smiled. "One of the sailors told me that the storm lasted two and a half days," he said. "It seemed more like two and a half weeks."

He played a short trill on his flute, and Rebekah listened. When he took the instrument away from his lips, she said, "I made a promise to myself during the storm. When I get to America I'm going to have an education and make something of myself. That's what this journey is all about for me."

Aaron's smile was endearing. "I thought about what you urged me to do, too," he said. "I won't give up my music."

Rebekah held up the little finger on her right hand and crooked it. "Give me your little finger," she said. When Aaron's little finger was crooked inside hers she told him, "We've made a promise to ourselves and to each other. Make a wish, and this will seal it."

Aaron took a deep breath and said, "I know that Nessin must have told you about my family. Someday I'll show up on your doorstep, Rebekah, and your parents won't send me away."

Rebekah looked up into Aaron's eyes. Then she tightened her finger and gave another tug. "Make your wish," she said. "God will help us face the future."

CHAPTER TEN

✦ ✦ ✦

THE voyage continued. The relatively smooth weather made Rebekah and the other passengers in steerage thankful that the ship was still afloat so they accepted the occasional closing of the hatches in choppy seas without complaint. But many passengers *did* complain about the water, which began to taste sour, and about the meals, which became progressively more meager.

The smell of unwashed bodies and clothes grew more ripe, but it was understood that it would be impossible for any of them to be really clean until they had left the ship.

Three passengers in steerage grew so ill that they died during the voyage. At each death Rebekah joined in the united mourning. Common bonds had made these strangers a family, grateful that for a while the occasional noisy disagreements and arguments spawned by the miserable living conditions had been set aside.

During the voyage Rebekah, Rose, and Kristin felt closer and closer in friendship. It was not until a ship's officer announced they'd be arriving in New

York Harbor the next morning that the girls spoke of leaving each other.

"Surely the United States can't be so big that we won't see each other again," Rose said. "No matter how far apart we live, we'll meet each other someday, and in the meantime we'll write letters—many, many letters."

"I'll write and tell you all about our farm," Kristin said. "You can come and visit. I'll teach each of you how to milk a cow."

"We know how to milk a cow," Rebekah and Rose answered in unison, then burst out laughing.

Tears glistened in Kristin's eyes as she said, "First I had to leave my grandmother. I didn't think on this ship I'd make such good friends. We *will* see each other again. I know we will."

"Of course we will," Rebekah insisted, but her voice broke, and she felt a tear slide down her nose. She marvelled that she had already had the good fortune to meet Rose and Kristin. She was so glad that her grandfather had taught her English. Even though they were so different, and she never would have been friends with non-Jewish girls in Russia, she felt connected to Rose and Kristin as if she'd known them forever. She knew that the United States was a vast country. She wrote out Uncle Avir's address for Rose and Kristin, and Rose made two copies of her father's address in Chicago.

"I'll let you know where we settle as soon as we have an address," Kristin promised.

During the day the steerage passengers grew more and more quiet. Rebekah could feel fear seep through the ship like a chilling gray fog. She tried to convince herself that everything would go well, and they'd soon join Uncle Avir, but the anxiety settled upon her shoulders.

All around her mothers appraised their children with frightened eyes, and people haltingly expressed their concerns. What if that pain in the chest was not from nervousness, but a problem with the heart? What if the pallor was not from being cooped inside a hellhole for two weeks, but was actually a sign of an incurable illness? Would the slump of a shoulder, the droop of a jaw, or a nervous stammer be enough to cause the inspectors to refuse admittance?

There were no loud conversations and no arguments in the hold that night, yet very few people slept. Rebekah lay awake until very late, staring at the dim lantern that swung hypnotically back and forth with the movement of the ship, and she listened to the constant rustle of whispers, sighs, and soft murmurs as the passengers both searched for comfort and gave it in turn.

A blast of the ship's horn woke her, and she jumped from her bunk, startled and alert. Through the open hatch she could see that the sky was still dark, but it had that softly rubbed look that showed the first light of morning would soon be on its way.

The horn from another ship sounded in the distance, and around Rebekah the people who were stirring began to move more quickly. Rebekah noticed that her mother's cheeks were red with excitement. She'd decked herself in an embroidered blouse and skirt; Rebekah changed into her festive clothes as well, adding the long, lumpy jacket she was never without. She grabbed her shawl and without waiting for the others in her family to follow ran up to the deck.

The air was clear, a fading moon low in the sky, and far on the horizon Rebekah, by squinting, could barely make out a dark, pencil-thin, irregular shape of land.

Land! The United States! They had arrived!

She raced down the stairs to her family. "I saw land!" she cried, and she heard others pick up the word and bounce it like an echo throughout the hold.

"Come," Mordecai said picking up his bundles. "We must all go on deck and get our first glimpse of our new country."

Elias tugged his coat around him. "We'll see Avir soon," he said, "most probably by this evening, and our new life will begin."

Together the Levinskys picked up their belongings and went on deck.

As Rebekah reached for her mother's hand, she felt her brother Nessin take her other hand and hold it tightly. She looked up and smiled at him, realizing with surprise that even Nessin was afraid of what was to come.

The colors of the sky slid from gray into a pale blue, and small puffs of clouds in the eastern sky exploded with bright pinks and oranges. The ship entered a bay and suddenly was surrounded by other steamships, tall-masted ships with sails, barges, tugs, and boats both large and small. The main deck became crowded with the passengers from steerage jostling and shoving against each other. No one wanted to miss this first view of the United States.

Members of the ship's crew pushed their way through the crowd, handing out bills of lading to be attached to baggage. "Get your tickets out where they can be seen," they ordered; after the crew came a ship's officer with the manifest, checking every name. At his direction, a sailor then handed each passenger a stringed tag with a large printed number that corresponded to the number beside the passenger's name on the manifest. Below it was a handwritten number that identified the manifest page.

"Tie those tags to your clothing. Don't lose them. Those are your landing tickets," the sailor warned over and over.

A small commotion caught Rebekah's attention. A gate in the ship's railing had been opened, and she could see and hear a tugboat thump snugly against the side of the ship. A ladder was let down, and up from the tug clambered a handful of men in uniform.

"Inspectors!" people were whispering, and Rebekah's heart began to beat loudly.

One of the inspectors elbowed his way to the hatch and paused only long enough to hold a handkerchief over his nose before he descended. He soon bounded on deck again, asking one of the ship's officers, "Any signs of cholera among the passengers? Smallpox? Yellow fever?"

In spite of the officer's denial, the inspectors walked among the steerage passengers, looking intently into faces, stopping occasionally to peer into bloodshot eyes or order a mouth to "open wide." As an inspector approached, Rebekah tensed, but he gave the Levinskys only a cursory glance and moved on.

Someone near the rail shouted, "There she is! The statue! The Statue of Liberty!" and the passengers turned to see the imposing figure they were approaching. Standing tall on her pedestal, gleaming in the early light, the points of her crown like those on a star, the lady raised high her torch of liberty.

" 'Mother of Exiles,' the poet Emma Lazarus called her," Mordecai said. " 'Give me your tired, your poor, your huddled masses yearning to breathe free.' That's all of us. 'She lifts her lamp beside the golden door.' In the United States we will become people of dignity."

Rebekah spotted Rose and Kristin at the rail. Unable to bear the rush of excitement alone, she squeezed through the crowd until she reached them and wrapped her arms around them as the ship sailed past the Statue of Liberty.

Beyond the Statue of Liberty on the nearest shore were many buildings, but ahead of the ship an astounding series of tall, crowded buildings seemed to rise from the water. "That's New York City," a woman said, and Rebekah gasped.

That was New York City? Impossible! How could anyone live in gigantic buildings like that? She thought of her small village, and the land she left behind—the farms with small vegetable gardens near their back doors. Where were the meadows and trees? What had Uncle Avir brought them to? How would they survive?

CHAPTER ELEVEN

❖ ❖ ❖

WHEN the ship docked, the first- and second-class passengers, who had gone through a quick inspection aboard ship, trotted down the gangplank, free to enter New York City. But the steerage passengers were ordered in numerous languages to hurry and collect their baggage, then return to the deck. And *hurry*!

Hurry down the gangplank to the Customs Wharf for a quick examination of baggage. No one owned enough of value to make the need for a customs inspection worthwhile. Hurry to the ferryboats. Squeeze in tightly . . . even more tightly. And *hurry*! Rebekah, bent under her bundle of possessions slung across her back, wondered why they had to hurry just to stand still, crammed together, waiting to be told again to hurry.

Rebekah searched the crowd for Rose and Kristin. She didn't find them, but she saw Aaron standing near the rail, a rectangular wicker suitcase balanced easily on his shoulder. As she met his eyes he smiled, and she felt a surge of happiness.

The ferryboat ride was a short one. As it approached Ellis Island, with its ornate, tower-studded gateway, a crewman threw a line to a dockhand, and the boat was soon tied to the hawsers on the dock. A short gangplank was put into place and someone called, "This way! Hurry! Hurry!"

Rebekah winced, but she followed the others to an open area that was already jammed with people. "Now what do we do?" she mumbled aloud.

"We wait," a voice answered, and Rebekah looked up to see Rose. Joyfully, as though they'd been parted for years, they hugged each other.

"Uncle Jimmy and I were on the ferry ahead of yours," Rose said. "They have so many people to process on the inside of the building, we have to wait our turn out here."

Rebekah looked around. "Have you seen Kristin?"

"She and her family were taken inside."

They were silent for a moment. Then Rebekah said, "I wonder what the inspection will be like."

"For one thing, they'll ask many questions," her grandfather volunteered.

"What kinds of questions?"

"Questions like those the officials asked back in Hamburg, but also questions to show you are smart enough to take care of yourself."

Leah interrupted. "We all have learned that Mr. Theodore Roosevelt is the president of the United States."

"Will they ask us the name of their president?"

"I have no idea," Leah answered impatiently, "but would it hurt to know?"

As the morning passed, countless ferryboats ran back and forth from the piers to the island, depositing large numbers of immigrants from other ships. And now and then the doors to the huge brick building opened, gulping in those crammed nearest the doors, then closing again.

Rebekah expected to walk into the building with Rose, but Rose and her uncle were the last of the group ahead of them to enter. A guard thrust out an arm, barring the Levinskys' way, and the doors closed.

"I'm hungry," Sofia said.

Rebekah was, too. They hadn't eaten since the evening before, and it was now close to noon.

She stood on tiptoe and again searched the hundreds of faces, trying to find Aaron, but this time she was unsuccessful. Even though he had come across the bay on a later ferry, surely he would have arrived by this time. He had to be on Ellis Island.

In about forty minutes the doors opened again, and the guard shouted, "Step on through."

If I hear "hurry" just one more time, I'll . . . But Rebekah didn't have time to finish her thought before the guard said, "Come along now. And *hurry!*"

They were herded into a massive, high-ceilinged hall that occupied the entire width of the building. Officials instructed them, in loud voices that reverberated throughout the room, to make sure a bill of lading was attached to each piece of baggage, then to leave their things among the already huge pile of wicker cases, carpetbags, trunks, and lumpy rugs and blankets that were stuffed with personal possessions.

"Will our possessions be safe?" Leah whispered to Elias.

"Hush," Mordecai answered. "Don't ask questions. Just do as they said and put down your bundle."

"But what about Elias's sewing machine? It's valuable. I don't like to leave it here where we can't keep an eye on it."

"Leah," Mordecai said firmly, "do as they told us to do. We have no choice."

There was no time for Leah to protest, even if she had wanted to. The immigrants were directed into dozens of lines separated by metal railings, and although there were many more orders to hurry, the lines moved sluggishly.

"Mama, I'm hungry!" Sofia suddenly wailed in Yiddish.

As Leah bent to soothe her, a woman wearing a trim black coat and black feathered hat walked toward the Levinskys. "Are you Jewish?" she asked in Yiddish.

"Yes," Leah answered, not sure what to make of the question.

The woman smiled. "My name is Esther Greenberg, and I'm from the Hebrew Immigrant Aid Society. I'm here to help you." She opened the large canvas bag she carried on her left arm and pulled out a roll of fragrant rye bread, wrapped in paper. As she handed the roll to Sofia she said, "I wish I could feed all of you, right this moment, because I know how hungry you must be. At least I can tell you that in the dining hall upstairs, there is also a kosher kitchen. When you are taken there to be fed, all you have to do is tell them kosher food is what you want. They don't provide a very large noon meal, but you'll find plenty of sardines and rye bread."

Leah beamed, and Elias cried, "Kosher food again! How can we thank you!"

"You don't need to thank me," Mrs. Greenberg said. "One of our members is here every day, and

81

if you have any problems, don't hesitate to call upon us."

As Mrs. Greenberg left the Levinskys to greet another group of people, Mordecai grinned. "You see? This country is wonderful. We'll soon have our stomachs filled, and in a short time we'll meet Avir. He'll take us to our new home in New York City. We've done the right thing."

Slowly the lines of people moved toward a wide stairway. "Put your child down," a guard directed a woman with a two-year-old girl in her arms.

"But she's exhausted," the woman argued.

The guard shook his head. He looked exhausted, too. "I'm sorry," he said, "but everyone over the age of two has to walk. We have to make sure they can."

"Of course she can!" the woman said. Indignantly, she put her daughter on her feet.

The little girl jumped up and down, wailing and, as people turned to stare, the mother looked as though she had suddenly realized where she was. Fear widening her eyes, she tried to hush her daughter.

Rebekah knew what worried the woman. Passengers who had been through Ellis Island warned others who were planning to make the trip to do nothing to call attention to themselves. People who were boisterous, or who attempted to ease their tension with loud jokes, or who were noisy in any way were often rejected as being possible misfits in society.

The child quieted in response to her mother's whispered pleadings and began to climb the stairs.

Mordecai took Rebekah's arm for support, and they slowly followed the others in their family.

It was not until they reached the head of the stairs that Rebekah saw that a group of inspectors had been watching the arrivals. One of the inspectors stepped forward and asked Mordecai, "Why are you limping?"

Mordecai's eyes opened in surprise. "When I was young a horse kicked my leg. The wound soon healed, but I've limped ever since."

The inspector raised his hand to Mordecai's left shoulder and wrote a large letter *L* with chalk.

"What does this mean?" Mordecai asked.

"The *L* stands for lameness," the inspector said. "Your leg will be checked by one of our doctors after you have gone through the rest of the medical examination."

"I have lived with this limp for a long time," Mordecai began, but the inspector had turned away and was speaking to an elderly woman whose back was humped with age. Quickly he wrote a large letter *B* on her shoulder and moved on to another immigrant.

Mordecai's forehead wrinkled with worry. Rebekah was frightened, too, but she said, "Grandfather, this is nothing to be afraid of. A doctor will just look at your leg. That's all they want . . . just to take a look and make sure that you were telling the truth."

"Identification cards," an attendant called over and over. "Have them out where they can be stamped."

This process, at least, was a quick one, and Rebekah followed her family into the central gangway partitioned into aisles by more metal dividers. At the beginning of each aisle stood an immigration doctor. Rebekah could see other doctors standing about thirty feet down the aisles, where the dividers turned in a sharp right angle.

"Walk slowly," another attendant instructed the group. "Keep about ten to fifteen feet apart. And remove anything that covers your head."

Rebekah pulled off her kerchief, as did Sofia and their mother, and each of the men in the Levinsky family removed their black, brimmed hats.

"Take off the skullcap, too," the doctor said to Nessin, who was the first Levinsky in line. "We must look for scalp diseases." But instead of doing so he examined Nessin's face and turned his head to study his profile. "Move on," he ordered. "Let me see you walk."

The rest of the Levinskys passed the doctor's cursory examination with no trouble, even Jacob, who was thin and pale after his long bout with seasickness. The doctor sent Mordecai on for the rest of the examination, but Rebekah saw him stop and watch her grandfather carefully as he limped down the aisle.

Rebekah took Mordecai's hand and held it tightly, wanting to reassure herself that everything would turn out all right, but she was frightened.

The doctor who stood at the bend in the aisles checked scalps for favus, a highly contagious fungus. In addition, he felt throats, looking for possible goiters, and studied skin that was unusually flushed, asking, "Have you ever had trouble breathing? Any pains in your chest?" Rebekah saw that he had written with his stick of chalk on others ahead of them in line: an *H* for a heart and an *SC* for scalp. On a woman who was expecting a child he wrote *PG*, just as if her condition weren't obvious to everyone.

Rebekah sniffed, but her disdain turned to sudden fear as the doctor reached up to the shoulder of an angry man, who had begun to shout and wave his arms, and drew an *X* with a circle around it. An attendant pulled the man from the line and led him away.

"Ohhh!" Rebekah heard someone gasp. "That mark means insanity."

"What if the man was just angry?" Rebekah asked Mordecai. "What if the doctor asked him questions he couldn't understand?"

Mordecai sighed, and the two of them huddled closer to each other.

The doctor frowned at the mark on Mordecai's coat, and he peered at him closely as Mordecai answered questions and went through his physical examination.

At the end of the lines Rebekah saw other doctors standing, examining each immigrant's eyes. A large window was behind them, and the sunlight that poured through the window apparently helped the doctors in their examination.

The doctors spoke to each person in line, asking questions about eyesight. They peered into each pair of eyes. Then, with small instruments that looked like buttonhooks, they everted the eyelids, searching for signs of trachoma or other illnesses.

Sofia let out an indignant yelp and pulled away. "That hurts!" she complained.

"I know, but it's necessary," the doctor told her. "Now, be a good girl and stand still so I can examine your other eye."

"No!" Sofia said.

With a scowl, the doctor stared up at Leah, and she trembled. "Sofia! Do what the doctor tells you!" she cried out in a voice so terrified that Sofia obeyed without question.

As the doctor finished his examination of Sofia he wiped the buttonhook on a towel, dipped his fingers into an antiseptic solution, then went on to examine Leah. Again, he dipped his fingers and examined Rebekah. All of them, including Mordecai, passed the eye examination without question.

"*Now* can we eat?" Sofia demanded.

No one bothered to answer, since they were immediately directed into a new line. One at a time, the immigrants were seated opposite inspectors who sat behind a row of desks. As the inspectors filled out official-looking government forms they asked countless questions: What is your full name? Your age? Your sex? Are you married or single? What is your calling or occupation? Nationality? Are you a polygamist? Have you ever been in prison or an almshouse? Were you ever supported by charity?

Elias, as head of the family, was first, and he answered many questions that covered the rest of his family, but he hesitated when the inspector asked, "Do you have a job?"

"Yes," he said, then immediately, "No."

"Which is it?" the inspector asked.

"My brother lives in New York City," Elias told him. "He said he would get me a job and a place for my family to live, so I assume he has done this, but I don't know where or what the job is."

"What kind of work do you do?"

"I am a tailor."

"What is your brother's address?"

Elias told him, and the man shook his head sadly and said, "Will all of your family work with you?"

"I told you, I don't know what Avir has arranged for us." Elias seemed confused.

"Do you have at least twenty-five dollars apiece with you?"

"Only twenty-five? Yes," Elias said.

"May I see it?"

Rebekah removed her jacket and handed it to her father. With his fingernails he pulled some threads and opened a seam in the left side of the lining, then reached in and removed the packages of bills.

The inspector thumbed through the money and nodded. "Don't put it back into the jacket," he said. "Put it where you can reach it easily. There will be an American Express office near the railway ticket office on the first floor where you can exchange your money into United States currency."

Are we that close to passing the inspection? Rebekah wondered, and her heart jumped with excitement. She held out her arms for her jacket, and with it her father automatically handed her the packets of money. Rebekah tucked the money down into the deep pockets in her skirt.

Before long it was her turn. She could tell that the inspector mostly wanted to discover if she had any mental problems. She answered his questions quickly and in English, so the examination was a short one.

While the inspector was busy writing information on the government form, Rebekah became aware that at the next desk a young woman sat huddled over, barely mumbling answers to another inspector's questions. The inspector who was attempting to question her finally slid a group of wooden blocks in front of her. "Can you match these?" he asked.

As she looked up and stared blankly, he explained, "There are two circles, two rectangles, and two of a number of other shapes. To begin, can you put the circles together? The squares? Please put them where they belong."

The woman gingerly picked up a square block. She stared at it for a long while, then put it next to a circle. Then she put her hands in her lap and hunched over, staring at them.

"Thank you," the inspector said. With a weary sigh he pushed the blocks to one side, picked up his chalk, and drew an X on the left shoulder of her coat.

He motioned to an assistant, who helped the woman up and led her away. Rebekah shivered and hugged her arms, trying to get warm. An X and an X with a circle around it—those must be mental misfits even the Mother of Exiles couldn't accept.

The inspector hesitated when he questioned Mordecai. "Has the physical disability in your right leg ever made you unfit for any kind of work?"

"Farm work, yes," Mordecai answered and smiled. "But where are there farms in New York City?"

"What work do you plan to do in New York?"

"I am a scholar. I study the Talmud."

The inspector frowned. "Will you have a job that pays a salary?"

"No. That is, I don't think so, unless Avir has found some form of employment for me."

"What is your age, Mr. Levinsky?"

"Sixty-two."

This time the inspector scowled as though Mordecai had given a wrong answer. "What work does your son do?" he asked.

"He is involved in sewing garments."

"In a factory?"

"No. He has never mentioned a factory. He has written something about his own small business where he is in charge." Mordecai spoke proudly, but the inspector again shook his head.

"A sweatshop," he muttered.

"What is that?" Mordecai asked.

The man didn't answer. Instead, he asked, "Who paid for your passage?"

"My sons, Avir and Elias, did."

The inspector leaned forward and peered at Mordecai. "You couldn't pay the fare yourself? There seems to be a possibility that you could become a public charge."

"No!" Mordecai and Rebekah shouted together.

"Your son Avir lives in a section of the city which is crowded with people struggling to make a living, as your family will discover. We can't count on him to keep you from needing public assistance."

"He won't need public assistance," Rebekah insisted. "We'll all work. We'll take care of him."

"The Board of Special Inquiry will have to decide that," the inspector said. He immediately became busy signing papers and stamping them. He handed a fistful to Elias and said, "You, your wife, your daughters, and your sons have been accepted."

"What will happen to Mordecai?" Leah cried.

The inspector pinned a yellow ticket on Mordecai's coat and said to him, "Go through that door to my left. You will be taken to rooms where you will undergo further examinations. If you pass them, you can rejoin your family."

If? Rebekah reached out for her grandfather, but an assistant was already leading Mordecai through the door, and Mordecai, his head bowed and his shoulders sagging, did not look back.

CHAPTER TWELVE

❖ ❖ ❖

THE Levinskys were directed to the dining hall, a large room filled with rows of long wooden trencher tables and benches. None of them had eaten for a long time, and in spite of Leah's tears and the family's worry about Mordecai, they wolfed down the sardines, the boiled potatoes and carrots, and the thick slices of fresh rye bread.

But Rebekah's thoughts were a torment. How could the inspector even consider the possibility that Mordecai might need public assistance? What did he mean when he spoke about Uncle Avir's neighborhood and mentioned a sweatshop? Avir had written only about how well he and Aunt Anna lived in the United States.

"What shall we do?" Leah asked. "Is there anything we can do?"

"Nothing but wait until we are told the board's decision," Elias said glumly.

Rebekah sat up stiffly, as she remembered the woman who had come to speak to them. "There *is* something we can do," she told her parents. "Esther Greenberg told us the Hebrew Immigrant Aid Society would help us. All we have to do is find her. She'll know how we can help Grandfather."

Leah stopped crying. "In this huge crowd, how will we find her?"

Rebekah hesitated only a moment before she swung her feet over the bench. "There must be someone in charge, Father. Should I ask one of the guards?"

"Your English is best, so go ask," her father consented.

Rebekah asked a passing uniformed guard. "Wait here with your family," he ordered. "We'll tell Mrs. Greenberg that you want to talk to her."

Rebekah and her family waited for Mrs. Greenberg nervously, but it wasn't until Jacob had gulped down a second plate of food that Mrs. Greenberg appeared in the dining hall.

Taking time for only a hasty greeting, Leah explained the situation and asked in Yiddish, "Can you help Mordecai?"

"He is my father," Elias told Mrs. Greenberg. "He won't become a public charge. I can take care of him."

"I'll see what I can find out," Mrs. Greenberg told them.

"Could we see Grandfather? Could we talk to him?" Rebekah asked.

"The Board of Special Inquiry will not allow immigrants to talk to friends or relatives until they've made their decisions," Mrs. Greenberg answered. "But I'll do everything I can to help."

Leah gave a long sigh of relief, but Mrs. Greenberg said, "I don't want to give you false hope, Mrs. Levinsky. There is no telling what the board will decide. It is made up of three inspectors, not always the same ones. Some of them tend to be lenient, but others are very hard on people with physical disabilities. Lately, there has been a great deal of public objection to allowing so many immigrants into the United States, and the inspectors on the board have been more strict than usual."

"Why do they object to us?" Rebekah asked.

"They are afraid of having to support you," Mrs. Greenberg answered. She rested a hand on Rebekah's shoulder. "Don't look so worried. I'll see what the situation is, and I'll join you on the first floor. Take the stairs at the far end of the inquiry room. When you reach the first floor, pass the railroad ticket office and go to the waiting room. You'll find benches there where you can rest while you wait."

The Levinskys had reached the first floor and were on their way toward the waiting room when Rebekah spied Kristin and her parents and Rose and her uncle, who were carrying their baggage and making their way toward the opposite end of the hall. With a cry, she ran toward them and reported what had happened to Mordecai.

While Rose and Kristin dropped their bundles and hugged Rebekah in sympathy, Mrs. Swensen grew teary-eyed and said, "Oh, Rebekah, I'm sure they'll allow your grandfather to stay."

Mr. Carney broke in. "Everything depends on politics and politicians. It's who you know that counts."

"Uncle Jimmy!" Rose scolded, and he gave a sheepish grin.

"Sorry, Rebekah. I should think before I speak. Well, consider what I said to be just my own opinion and no one else's and hope for the best. Your grandfather's a smart man. He'll come through all right."

Mr. Swensen took a step forward. "We'd help you if we could, Rebekah, but there is nothing we can do." He glanced up at the large clock on a nearby wall and added, "And now it is time for us to leave. We have to take the next ferry to New Jersey so we can arrive at the railroad terminal on time to catch our train."

"Rosie needs to catch that same ferry," Mr. Carney said, and he put a hand on Rose's arm, guiding her toward the short stairway leading down from the main level.

Rose twisted her head toward him as the group moved along, Rebekah walked with them. "What do you mean 'Rosie needs to catch the ferry'? We're *both* taking it, aren't we, Uncle Jimmy?"

"Ah, now, Rosie," he said, never breaking stride as he shoved a train ticket into her hands, "I didn't find the time to tell you that I've got friends in New York City I'd like to visit for a while. You're a big girl, almost grown, and perfectly well able to travel to Chicago by yourself."

"By myself?" Rose cried, her eyes huge.

A whistle on one of the ferries at the dock just outside the building tooted three long blasts.

"That's our boat! Hurry!" Mr. Swensen said and loped down the stairs.

Rebekah, Rose, and Kristin threw their arms around each other in one last, awkward hug.

"Hurry! Kristin! Come now!" Mr. Swensen shouted.

Mrs. Swensen grabbed Kristin's arm and pulled

her away. They dashed down the stairway, Rose right behind them.

At the foot of the stairway Rose wailed, "Uncle Jimmy!" at Mr. Carney, but he gave her no more than a jaunty wave before he strode off to the left, disappearing through the doorway under the sign: *To the New York Ferry.* Rose threw one last, aching glance at Rebekah before she turned to the right and ran after the Swensens and the boat to New Jersey.

Rebekah watched her friends disappear. There was so much she wanted to tell them, so much she hadn't had time to say. Heedless of the baggage-laden people who pushed around her as they clumped down the stairs, she leaned her head against the wall, tears streaming unchecked down her cheeks.

A hand touched her shoulder, startling her, and she stiffened. "Aaron!" she cried as she looked up. "Oh, Aaron! I'll never see Kristin and Rose again!"

Aaron pulled Rebekah to one side, away from the traffic on the stairway, and held her so that she could cry against his shoulder.

"Remember what you told me about making things happen," Aaron said. "Just promise yourself that you *will* see them again and believe it will happen."

Rebekah stepped away from Aaron and wiped her eyes. "I wasn't crying only because I had to say good-bye to them," she said. "I'm terrified of what may happen to Grandfather." She told Aaron about Mordecai's detention and about Esther Greenberg's offer to try to help.

"I'll wait with you," Aaron said.

Rebekah knew that her mother had enough worries at the moment. There was no telling what she would think or the questions she'd ask if her daughter brought a strange young man to sit with them. Nessin might tell Mama what he had told Rebekah about Aaron's family. No.

"I can't let you do that," she said. "Your father will be expecting you. He may come to meet you."

Aaron pulled a slip of paper from one of his pockets and held it up. "He sent me only his address and directions in finding his place," he told Rebekah.

"But he'll know that your ship has docked," Rebekah insisted. "He'll worry if you don't arrive. Please go, Aaron."

He hesitated, then nodded. "Then stand at the head of the stairway and wave to me when I go. Someone told me these are called the Stairs of Separation, but they won't be for us."

"Aaron," Rebekah began, but he interrupted.

"And smile, Rebekah," he said. "I want to remember your smile until I see you again."

"Oh!" she cried. "My Uncle Avir's address! Wait until I write it down for you."

"I have it," Aaron answered. He bounded down the stairs and turned toward the left, waving and smiling at her until he disappeared through the door that led to the New York Ferry.

Rebekah's smile faded, and she wondered if she could ever be happy again. Tired and discouraged, she walked past the piles of baggage and past the crowd of people who were pushing their way up to the railway ticket counter. On the walls behind them she could see posters telling the wonders of other states in the United States—Nebraska, Texas, and California—so distant and strange she couldn't even picture them.

When Rebekah reached the waiting room she was shocked as she saw her father's face sag as though he were an old man and her mother droop with exhaustion. Even Nessin was subdued, and Sofia slept—Jacob's arm around her. Silently, Rebekah sat with them. Leah didn't speak. She simply reached out and squeezed Rebekah's hand.

It was a long, agonizing hour later when Esther Greenberg came to sit with them. "Your father's case will probably come up for examination in a few hours," she told Elias. She held out a folded paper. "I've written the address of the Hebrew Immigrant Aid Society offices for you. It's on Broadway in the Lower East Side of New York City, probably close to where you'll be living. Please don't hesitate to visit us if you need any kind of help."

"Thank you," Elias answered, taking the paper and tucking it into a pocket.

"Can we see Grandfather?" Rebekah asked. All she wanted or needed right now was for her grandfather to be released.

"Only after his case has been decided." Mrs. Greenberg looked away for a moment and sighed. Then her back straightened and she said, "I know this is difficult for you. It is for many people who must wait and wonder if they may stay or if they must return."

"Do many have to return?" Jacob asked.

"Just a little over two percent," Mrs. Greenberg said softly.

"How many emigrants come to Ellis Island?" Rebekah asked.

"Many," Mrs. Greenberg answered. Her eyes met

Rebekah's. "Sometimes up to five thousand people a day."

Two percent of five thousand people? Two percent would mean at least one hundred people a day who were turned away! Rebekah's throat grew tight, and her stomach began to hurt. Mrs. Greenberg was preparing them to accept the worst.

CHAPTER THIRTEEN

❖ ❖ ❖

FOR hours Rebekah and her family waited without word, until finally another volunteer from the Hebrew Immigrant Aid Society told them to follow him and took them to a room with a large cage-like section that was constructed from wide-holed wire mesh.

Mordecai was seated with other detainees on one of the wooden benches inside the mesh, and when he saw his family he painfully got to his feet and limped over to the side of the cage. "I have been rejected," he told them in a voice hoarse with pain. "I am being sent back."

"Not to Russia!" Leah cried.

"No," Mordecai said. "They will let me leave the ship at Liverpool on a temporary visit. My cousins . . . Samuel, Abraham . . . they are good men. I know I can stay with them until I decide what to do."

As the other members of her family tried to comfort one another, Rebekah moved close to speak to Mordecai in a low voice. Her fingers trembled as she gripped the wires. "Grandfather, we will work hard and save our money and send it to you so you can travel to the United States again."

Mordecai shrugged and shook his head. "What good would it do? I'd be rejected again."

"Not if you travel in second class, instead of steerage," she pleaded. "Buy a good suit and a hat that a second-class passenger would wear. The inspectors will accept you because they'll think you are well off and can support yourself. Remember what we heard on the ship?"

"Little one," Mordecai said tolerantly, "that would take more money than the family can earn for quite some time."

"This will help," Rebekah whispered. She reached into her skirt, pulled out one of the packets of money, and stuffed it through the wire mesh. "Take it, quickly! Hide it!"

Startled, Mordecai did as she told him, but he said, "That is the family's money. You'll need it."

"Uncle Avir will help us." Trying to keep her voice from shaking, Rebekah begged, "Grandfather, promise me that you'll return in second class."

He smiled. "I'll do my best, and I shall try to look like a gentleman."

Rebekah attempted to return his smile. "When you return to the United States, Grandfather, I'll be waiting for you at the dock."

Rebekah knew she had to make herself believe that what she had promised her grandfather would come true. If she couldn't believe, she'd never be able to bear parting from him.

"Rebekah, my little scholar," Mordecai said, "in return I ask a promise of you. Since I will not be with you to help your family become used to this new country with ways that may seem strange or even frightening, I need you to do it for me. You are a sensible girl. Even though the change will be difficult for you, as well as for your family, I know I can count on you to know what is right and to do what is best. Do I have your promise?"

"Of course you do, Grandfather!" Rebekah insisted, but she wondered, how could she know what was best for her family? She had no idea what lay ahead.

Elias joined them. "When will you leave?" he asked his father.

"The day after tomorrow," Mordecai answered.

"Then we will wait here with you."

"And talk now and then through this wire screen? No," Mordecai said. "Avir will be waiting for you. The time for us to part is now. On this matter I insist."

The Levinskys clustered around for a last, tearful farewell before Mordecai hefted his small bundle of possessions and walked through a doorway that led to another part of the building.

"Grandfather!" Rebekah fought against a creeping, clawing panic. Mordecai would return. He would! Maybe within a year. Maybe two . . .

Or would she ever see him again? A sob rose in her throat, and she pressed her hands against the burning pain in her stomach.

Heartsick, the Levinskys straggled to the baggage room to claim their possessions. They shouldered them—Nessin carrying the sewing machine—and made their way to the American Express office to change their money into United States currency. It was there that Rebekah confessed to what she had done.

Leah gasped. "We had very little money in the first place! Now what will we do?"

Wrinkles of worry etched Elias's forehead, but he smiled wearily and said, "What's done is done. My father has blessed and helped us by teaching us English. Who knows if Rebekah's impulsiveness was wrong or right? This is a difficult parting—as hard as our leaving our home."

But Leah persisted. "With half our money gone, how will we buy food?" she asked. "How will we pay for a place to live? What is going to happen to us now?"

To Rebekah's surprise Jacob spoke up. "Mama," he said, "we have so much to worry about, one thing more won't matter. Uncle Avir will be on hand to guide us, and somehow we'll survive."

"We may all go hungry," Leah grumbled.

"Being hungry could never be as bad as being seasick," Jacob answered. "We're here to exchange the money that's left, so why are we wasting time? Why don't we exchange it now and take the next ferry to New York?"

On the ferry Rebekah glanced at the other members of her family, their faces drooping with misery. Everyone had arrived with such hope, and this last ferry trip to Battery Park should have been one of joy and excitement, but it was not.

The volunteer from HIAS had sent a message to Avir, and he was waiting for them at Battery Park when the ferry docked. Avir looked much as Rebekah remembered him—a thin, wiry man with a short, thick beard and mustache. As the Levinskys approached, his eyes darted from one to another, and he called to Elias, "Where's Father?"

There was much hugging and explaining and a fresh flow of tears from Leah, as Elias explained that Mordecai had been refused admittance to the United States.

Avir blew his nose loudly into his handkerchief, and his voice broke. "I never thought this would happen. I wanted him—all of you—safely out of Russia, away from the czar and his cossacks."

"Grandfather will stay with cousins in England until he comes to America again," Rebekah hurried to tell Uncle Avir. "Others have come back in second class and been accepted."

Avir sighed. "It would take a long time to save enough money for second class."

"You wrote that you are doing well here in America," Elias said. "If the country is as kind to us as well, surely it won't take long to save the price of second-class fare."

Embarrassment washed over Avir's face, turning his nose and cheeks a dull red. "Life is better than it was in the shtetl," he said, "but did I say I was rich? Never! There is plenty of piecework to be had, but in order to earn enough money to eat well we must work long, hard hours."

Leah sighed and said, "We will do what must be done and manage to put as much as we can aside."

Avir pulled out a shiny silver pocket watch, glanced at it, then led the family to a horse-drawn trolley, grandly paying their fares, and they rode through heavy traffic of horse-drawn buggies, carts, and heavy drays to their new home in the city.

At their stop Rebekah followed the others from the trolley, made her way to the sidewalk, and slowly turned in a circle, staring open-mouthed at the crowds of people, many of them hurrying, as though on their way to work. Some of the men were dressed in dark suits and white shirts with stiffly starched collars, but many wore the traditional black, broad-brimmed hats and long coats familiar to Rebekah. Most of the women were dressed in kerchiefs and shawls, but a few young women wore coats with nipped-in waists and hats with broad brims and flat-topped crowns perched squarely on their heads.

Who were these smartly dressed women? Rebekah wondered. *Where were they going? Was it possible that some of them were students? Is this how women students dressed?*

"Come along, Rebekah," Uncle Avir called, and she ran, her bundle bouncing against her back as she caught up to her family.

"Where are we?" she asked.

"Near Grand Street. This is called the Lower East Side."

"Where is our home?"

"You'll soon be there," Avir answered. "There is a flat across the hall from ours, and fortunately it just became available."

"What is a flat?"

"You ask too many questions," Avir said, but Rebekah didn't mind. It was too noisy and crowded on the street to carry on a shouted conversation with any success, and she was more interested in what she was seeing than in whatever Uncle Avir could tell her.

They turned a corner and entered a street that was like a bazaar, but it was far more cluttered and crowded than market day in the shtetl at home. Tat-

tered, faded awnings hung over the narrow store-
fronts that lined the ground floors of countless brick
and wooden multistoried buildings. Wrought-iron
balconies and fire escapes jutted out below windows,
and ornately carved lamp poles held aloft electric
light globes. Peddlers whose pushcarts were mounded
with fruit and vegetables, drivers of horse-drawn delivery carts and wagons, stall keepers displaying
food, dishes, and baby clothes, and harried pedestrians—bags and baskets over their arms—noisily
fought for space. People shouted at each other in
Yiddish, Hebrew, and English. Adding to the general
commotion, crated chickens and geese kept up a
cackling, honking din. The air was thick with mingled smells of dust, horse dung, fish, and newly
baked loaves of bread.

"Gutes frucht!" a peddler yelled at Leah, and he
waved something narrow and yellow in her face.

Avir turned and grinned at Leah, then shook his
head at the peddler. "That piece of fruit is a banana," he said. "Someday you'll have to eat one."

"Is it kosher?" Leah asked.

Avir's eyebrows rose in surprise. "Kosher? In this
neighborhood you don't need to worry."

"Bargain!" another peddler screamed at Leah.
"Ten cents, and I give you enough tomatoes for your
whole family!"

"What is this place?" Rebekah shouted to her
uncle.

"Hester Street," he said, and he gave a jerk of his
head toward the right. "One more block, and we
are home."

As they managed to progress through the traffic
they were shouted at from both sides. "Bluefish! Buy

now! Good bargain! Fresh cakes! Collar buttons, suspenders, handkerchiefs!"

"Look!" Sofia shouted and pointed at a man wearing a wobbling tower of hats, one inside the other.

"Old clothes. I buy old clothes," he chanted as he passed, giving the Levinskys an appraising look that quickly slid into a lack of interest.

Uncle Avir made another turn and led them a few blocks down a narrow street. Refuse littered the sidewalk and clumped where it had blown against row after row of outdoor steps that led down to the street from identical stained and peeling front doors. Avir ushered them into the fourth building from the corner and up a dark, narrow, staircase to the third floor. He stopped in front of one door and opened it wide.

Rebekah had expected rooms that would be homelike, with comfortable chairs and a table and maybe a few rugs on the floor; she was astounded when she saw at least a half dozen people inside the room, all of them hunched over fabric or sewing machines. Dark woolen cloth was everywhere—on laps, on tables, and on the floor—and the lint from the cloth covered everything and everyone with a fine black dust. A dingy, colorless fringe decorated the lower edges of the raised window shades, but aside from the sconces that held gas lamps, there were no pictures or paintings to break the monotonous, faded wallpaper.

"This is my home and my shop!" Avir announced proudly, but he made no move to introduce them to his workers. A presser and a seamstress glanced up but quickly went back to their work when they caught Avir's eye on them. "I've arranged to rent the flat across the hall," he said, "so I can set up another shop like this for you to manage, Elias."

Elias tried to talk, then cleared his throat and tried again, but still the words were faint. "I—I could not manage a shop, Avir," he said. "I am a tailor. If I could get a job somewhere as a tailor . . ."

"New York City is full of tailors," Avir said. "And those who work in factories make less than ten dollars a week. Besides the coats my workers are making, I've got a new contract to make three hundred pairs of boys' pants, which I'm going to subcontract to you. I have to pay outside help to press, baste, finish, trim, and so on, but with your entire family here to help with all those jobs, you could easily clear a profit of thirty dollars for the week's work!"

He took his brother's arm and peered into his face. "With a shop in your flat, your whole family to work for you, and rent just six dollars a week, think of how successful you can be, Elias!"

"This is not the kind of work I am used to doing," Elias answered.

"Don't you understand, Elias? This and factory work are all that is available for us!" Avir said. "Consider yourself fortunate that I've set this up for you. There are plenty of people out there who are after these jobs. Operators get fifteen dollars a week, finishers ten, basters twelve."

"Not everyone in my family will work Avir," Elias began. "Jacob has his religious studies. We will look for a rebbe who is a good teacher, for a yeshiva . . ."

"For a while Jacob can postpone his studies," Avir said. "You have to get established, Elias. I'm trying to help you do so, and you'll soon understand I know the best way."

Rebekah glanced from Jacob's shocked expression to the workers in the crowded room. It was hot, with steam rising from irons at which a young man toiled, without his shirt on. Sweat rolled down faces, necks, and backs; arms glistened in the heat.

This is a sweatshop, Rebekah thought, and her stomach clutched in revulsion. This is not what they'd come to America for! Not to live like this!

"Elias, I have made a thriving business for myself," Avir said. "It may not be just what you expected, but at least we live in freedom, safely away from pogroms and the cossacks. Am I not right?"

Elias nodded agreement, but Rebekah glanced at her mother, whose face was pale. Her father's eyes had dulled. Jacob looked as sick as he had on the ship. But Nessin's lip curled defiantly, and Rebekah knew he wasn't about to accept this life either.

"It can be a rewarding and successful business for those who master it," Avir continued. "The manufacturers have piecework which must be done. They call for bids on each order. Maybe it's six hundred men's coats, maybe one hundred women's shirts. Usually, the manufacturers accept the lowest bid. The trick is in coming just under the others with a penny here, a penny there—without going too low. The profits are not large, but with quantity and careful management I have created a successful business." He swept his arm in a proud gesture around the room. "It will be the same for you, my brother."

Avir didn't give Elias time to answer but went on: "The manufacturers establish deadlines for each order of piecework to be completed, and these deadlines allow very little time. We work from six in the morning until nine at night to meet the deadlines. Only those who can win the bids and meet the deadlines have any chance to survive in this business."

Leah's expression was one of bewilderment, but to maintain face she said, "Enough talk of business for now, Avir. Where is your wife, Anna? It's been such a long time . . . I'm eager to see her."

"She's cooking our evening meal," Avir said. "She's preparing enough to share with you, and when she brings it to you, you'll have a short time in which to greet her before she must return to work."

"Brings it? Where? What do you mean?"

Without answering, Avir suddenly shooed them back into the hallway and shut the door. Across the hall he opened the door to an empty, dirty string of rooms. "Come," he called and strode through to the kitchen in back, his footsteps echoing. "Put down your baggage. This is your new home."

The Levinskys sadly looked at one another, but followed Avir into a good-sized kitchen, which contained a black cast-iron coal stove, a corner sink with a single cold-water faucet, and a table with six chairs. The wooden floors were stained and sticky, but Avir gave them only a cursory glance and shrugged. "Once Leah and Rebekah scrub these floors clean, this will be your favorite room in the house."

At least the kitchen had sunlight streaming through the window, Rebekah noticed. With the exception of the pair of windows facing the street, the windows in the other two rooms faced only the brick wall of the building next door.

"I need the privy," Sofia demanded. "Where is it?"

"Outside in back," Avir said, and Leah took her daughter's hand, hurrying her out of the room.

"We'll outfit the other rooms with beds and sofas and tables—lots of tables to work on," Avir continued. "There are secondhand-furniture salesmen with carts." Avir stopped and looked expectantly at Elias. "You have enough money with you to buy the furniture and extra sewing machines you'll need, haven't you?"

"We do not have much money left," Elias said. He reached into his pocket and removed the folded United States currency he'd been given at the American Express office on the island. "We gave some to Father when he was detained."

Avir's eyebrows rose as he thumbed through the bills, removing two of them before he returned the rest to Elias. "At least you can pay for the first week's rent," he said. "I am your brother. I will lend you the money to buy your furniture and the sewing equipment you'll need."

"Thank you," Elias said quietly. "You've done a great deal. I don't know what I was expecting, but we can't go back. We will do what must be done."

So. Her father had decided. Rebekah ached at seeing the despair in his face. This had been a frightening change for her parents—for *all* of them. The life Uncle Avir had arranged for them in New York City was so different from their quiet lives. But did they have to agree to everything he said? If only Grandfather had been admitted to America. What would he have done? What would he want her to do?

Rebekah took a deep breath and said, "Father, what about Jacob's yeshiva studies? Couldn't he help after his studies each day?"

Both her father and uncle looked at her with surprise, but Elias's eyes shone warmly. He told his brother, "What Rebekah says is fair. We will all work hard to repay your loan as quickly as possible. But Jacob will work after he has come from yeshiva and done his studies each day."

"Very well, then." Avir shrugged.

By this time Leah and Sofia had returned. "If you have some lye soap and cleaning utensils we can borrow, Rebekah and I will get to work on this . . . this flat, as you call it," Leah said. "Then we'll go to Hester Street and shop for food and dishes."

Avir looked pleased and nodded briskly. "It will all work out well for you . . . for all of us," he said, and he began to explain to Elias how the shop would be set up and run.

Rebekah didn't listen. Noise from the streets below became a background of discordant sounds that went on, and on, and on. Rebekah wanted to cover her ears, to scream, to cry, but she couldn't. She had lost her grandfather, she had surely lost the opportunity to go to school, she had lost the friends she had made on board ship, and she and her family seemed to be left with a horrible life of unending drudgery, noise, and dirt.

In desperation, she walked to the front windows and raised them high. The din from the streets increased, but a cool breeze blew into the room. As it touched Rebekah's face, it reminded her of the breezes from the sea. With it came memories of Mordecai, Aaron, Kristin, and Rose. She stood a little straighter.

Rebekah could accept the fact that she and her family might have to follow the program Uncle Avir had arranged for them, at least until he had been repaid, but she knew that there were other ways to live—happier, more comfortable ways. Surely America was not a place made up of people living miserable lives. In Russia, people lived with more and less. She would find a way to make a better life in this land. She only had hope, but she wouldn't give that up.

CHAPTER FOURTEEN

❖ ❖ ❖

UNCLE Avir took Nessin away with him, and Nessin returned with a broom, scrub brushes, a bucket, and a large, sloshing jar of pungent, acrid-smelling lye soap. Before Rebekah changed to a work dress, she turned to her father.

"Papa," she said, "we cannot sew here until the rooms are clean. Perhaps while Mama and I work you can visit the people at the HIAS office and ask them to help you find a yeshiva for Jacob? You have the address. And Mrs. Greenberg told us they'd help us in any way."

Elias slowly straightened his shoulders and began to relax. "A good idea," he said. He fished in his pocket for the piece of paper. When he had found it, he nodded to Jacob. "Come with me. We'll see what these people can tell us."

Soon after they had left, Nessin edged toward the door. "I'll take a look around and find out more about this place," he said.

"You can stay and help us," Leah said.

"That's women's work," Nessin complained. He made a dash out the door, and they could hear his footsteps clattering down the stairs.

With an indulgent shrug Leah searched through one of the family's bundles of clothing and pulled out two aprons, handing one to Rebekah. They tied them over their long skirts, rolled up their sleeves, and got to work.

By the time they had finished, the walls, the floors, and the kitchen furnishings reeked with the acid smell of lye soap, but everything was spotlessly clean.

Anna, round as a dumpling squeezed in at the middle, appeared bearing an iron pot filled with a fragrant mixture of chicken and vegetables. Squeaking with cries of delight, she hurried to the kitchen, put down the pot, and threw her arms around Leah. "Oh, how glad I am you're here!" she exclaimed and burst into tears.

Anna swept Sofia close, too, laughing with her, sobbing, talking, and snuffling. "Come here, Rebekah! Rebekah, my darling!" Aunt Anna shouted, and Rebekah joined the hugging, remembering with happiness how she had always loved her aunt.

Anna finally drew away. "We have much to talk about," she said, "but there are other things to bring over—dishes and utensils and challah bread, fresh out of the oven, and a potato kugel, especially for little Sofia! Come with me. You can all carry something."

By the time they returned to their flat, Elias and Jacob had returned. Nothing was said about the success of their errand, but both men glowed with such expressions of joy and satisfaction that Rebekah knew one problem had been solved.

It was not until the meal was finished that Anna suddenly looked surprised and asked, "Here we have been talking and talking, and I haven't stopped to ask, where is Nessin?"

"He went out to look at the neighborhood," Leah said. "If the food is cold when he comes in to eat, it's nobody's fault but his own."

Anna smiled. "Nessin must be nearly grown," she began. "Is he still getting in and out of mischief?"

Just then Avir appeared in the doorway, his outdoor hat on his head. "Elias," he said, "you and I are going to talk to some men who have used furniture for sale, and I have heard where we can get two good, used Singer sewing machines to add to your own."

As Elias quickly stood, wiping his mouth on his napkin, Avir said to his wife, "You and Leah will have time to talk later tonight, Anna. Right now you're needed to lend a hand with the finishing on some coats."

Anna jumped to her feet even faster than Elias had, and Rebekah watched the three of them leave. There was such a constant demand with the business that already she resented it. Life shouldn't be all work. There should be time to think, to study, to dream. She thought she sounded like her grandfather and hoped he was safe.

"Let me tell you what happened," Jacob said in a rush of excitement. "They were very helpful at the HIAS office. They sent us to the synagogue on East Broadway to speak with a Rebbe Schwartz. I am enrolled in his yeshiva and will start my studies with him on Monday. The cost is much less than Papa had thought it would be."

He waited until Rebekah and Leah were through shrieking and hugging him, and said, "The people of HIAS told us about other schools, too. There is a public school for younger children less than six blocks away, where Sofia can be enrolled. In New York children *must* be sent to school. And, nearby, there is a Hebrew school she can attend later in the afternoon. Nessin can study English in evening classes, and when he's ready to pass his exams for all his subjects in English, he can enroll in City College."

Leah sucked in her breath. "How can we possibly manage the expense of all this study?"

"Mama," Jacob said, "the public schools in this country are *free*! The classes at the center are free for those who otherwise couldn't afford them. And the Hebrew school for Sofia will cost just a few pennies a week."

Free! Rebekah thought. She hadn't dared to dream that classes would be free!

Leah put her hands to her cheeks. "All this schooling can't be possible, Jacob. It is a luxury even for free right now. Avir has contracted for a great deal of work, and we must do it."

"But not Sofia!" Rebekah cried, her heart hammering with excitement. "And Nessin's school would meet in the evening, not during the day!"

"That's right, Mama," Jacob said.

Swept up in her children's excitement, her eyes sparkling, and her cheeks reddening, Leah said, "Well, then, we will see that Nessin takes evening classes and Sofia is enrolled in public school. Hebrew School will come later. Your father and I need to think, to plan. This is all happening too fast."

"Will there be school for *me*, Mama?" Rebekah

clasped her hands together tightly under her chin and held her breath, hoping . . . hoping . . .

Leah's eyes widened. "You, Rebekah? But you are a fifteen-year-old girl—nearly grown. The schools are for young men and children."

Rebekah reached for her mother's hands and held them. "Mama, I want an education more than I've ever wanted anything in my whole life. I want to be a teacher. Someday I want to go to college, too—to the City College Jacob told us about . . ."

Jacob interrupted. "City College is for males only."

Rebekah begged, "Please, Mama? Please say I can go to evening classes with Nessin and prepare for training to become a teacher."

The amazement in Leah's expression faded, and she stared at Rebekah with bewilderment and sorrow. "Rebekah," she said, "what are you thinking of? We will all be working long hours. How can you be so selfish that you'd ask your parents to spend money on an education for *you*? In a few years you'll marry and raise children, and an education would be nothing but a useless waste of money."

"No!" Rebekah cried as her dream became even more important. "I'll need an education." She fought to regain control and added in a calmer voice, "Even if someday I do decide to marry and raise a family, I'd be a better wife and mother if I had an education."

Leah's eyes narrowed with hurt, and Rebekah winced, knowing there was nothing she could say to repair her heedless words.

"I don't believe what I am hearing from my own daughter," Leah answered. "*If* you decide to marry?

If you marry? Of course you will marry when your father and I think it is the proper time to arrange it. Would you want to spend your life dependent on your brother Nessin, living in his home and helping his wife as a penniless old maid who had to be taken care of?"

Rebekah spoke quietly, aware that her mother would be upset. "With an education I wouldn't have to be taken care of, Mama. If I were a teacher I could support myself and even help give money to you and Papa."

Leah struggled to her feet, angrily smoothing down her skirts as she walked away from the table. "You don't know what you are talking about," she said. "I don't know where you got such foolish ideas. I don't want to hear any more of this talk."

"But, Mama . . ."

"Hush, Rebekah. I have too much on my mind. You have always been my good girl. Don't turn on me now."

"Could we talk later?"

"Very well, later. We will talk about it at some time in the future."

Rebekah nodded. Perhaps nothing she could say at this time would change her mother's mind, but she was determined not to give up.

At that moment the door burst open, and Nessin thundered through the flat and into the kitchen. His collar was torn, his hair hung over his forehead, his yarmulke was gone, and a large bruise colored his chin.

Leah gasped and cried, "Nessin! What has happened to you?"

"Italians," Nessin answered. He turned on the

118

water spigot and held his head under it. Then he shook his hair, as though he were a puppy, and groped for a hand towel to dry his face.

"What is that supposed to mean?" Leah demanded. "You have been fighting, haven't you?"

"I had to," Nessin said, "or a gang might have killed me."

"Where did this happen?" Jacob asked. He handed a towel to his brother.

"In their ghetto," Nessin answered. His glance shifted from Jacob to Leah. "I was just walking, just looking around. I didn't know there were boundaries—Jews in one place, Italians in another, Irish over there. But there are, and I walked into a street owned by an Italian gang, and they chased me." He rubbed his chin. "They were fast, too. Faster than I was."

"You were alone?" Jacob asked.

"At first, but I was almost back in Jewish territory so I began yelling in Yiddish, and a couple of boys heard, and they came to help me." For the first time Nessin smiled, and he rubbed the knuckles of his right hand. "We put up a good fight, and some of them are going to remember it."

"Ach!" Leah cried. "There will be no more fighting!"

"Not unless they ask for it by coming into our territory," Nessin insisted. "Now I've got friends here, and we'll look out for each other."

"You're in a gang?" Jacob asked quietly. He stopped abruptly as Nessin gave him a warning look, but Leah was so upset she hadn't heard Jacob.

"Nessin! Listen to me!" his mother demanded. "I said there will be no more fighting, and I meant it."

119

"But if I have to defend myself . . ."

"You will not have to defend yourself if you are busy with work during the day and lessons in the evening," she said. "Pay attention and Jacob will tell you about the night-school classes and a place called City College."

Nessin listened, but he didn't look pleased. When Jacob had finished, Nessin muttered, "Work all day and school all night? I've got to have some time for fun."

Oh, why couldn't Nessin have been the girl and I have been the boy, so that I could have the education he doesn't want? Rebekah wondered. *It isn't fair!*

"Mama," Jacob said as he darted a pointed glance at Rebekah, "when are you and Rebekah going shopping for food?"

"Food!" Leah said, her mind diverted to a more immediate problem. "Of course we must buy food, and candles, and wine for Shabbas. There is supper to prepare, bread to bake . . ." For a moment her eyes narrowed with fear, and she asked, "Rebekah, you can speak English, but do you think you can deal with the merchants? How will we know if their prices are fair? What if they try to cheat us?"

Rebekah took her mother's hand. Leah had always been secure in knowing how to take care of her family, but it was in a country where she understood the customs and the language.

"It's all right, Mama," Rebekah said. "The two of us will manage. We may make a few mistakes, but it won't take long for us to learn the merchants' ways."

Only a few minutes later Rebekah and her mother

had changed into street clothes, added their shawls and kerchiefs, and begun their walk to Hester Street.

As they dove into the crowded cluster of carts and shops Rebekah stopped to look at the bright-colored fruit in the nearest stalls. A large bunch of bananas lay in a golden mound. "I wonder what those taste like," she said.

"Don't bother to wonder," Leah said as she nervously eyed the shouting, clamoring people around them. "They're strange-looking things. No matter what Avir said, they may not be kosher."

The owner of the cart turned from a customer and answered in Yiddish, "Kosher? Since when haven't bananas been kosher?"

Leah gulped in surprise, then stammered, "You speak Yiddish."

The man made a wide sweep with both arms and said, "Everyone here is Yiddish. What do you expect, you come to a Yiddish community? You are from Romania? Poland? Never had a banana? Buy bananas. You'll like them. Buy potatoes. I'll give you the lowest price on potatoes."

"How much are your potatoes?" Leah countered and when he told her she answered, "I'll look around."

"My prices are lowest. I'll match any other price you're offered," he insisted, and the two of them entered into a spirited discussion of the prices of not only potatoes, but onions, cabbage, and carrots.

When the peddler finally countered with a final price and insisted he could go no lower, Leah turned to Rebekah and asked, "How much would this American money be at home?"

At home. Rebekah's throat tightened as the words called up a picture of the marketplace, of her mother's heaped market basket, and the warmth of the kitchen as her purchases were changed into mouth-watering stews and broths and fragrant loaves of bread. She and Chava would beg for a taste of bread, fresh from the oven and . . . Oh, how she longed for her friend Chava and for the comfort of her child-hood home.

"Rebekah?" her mother repeated, and Rebekah hurried to translate the amount.

Leah nodded with satisfaction, handed Rebekah the shopping money—instructing her to pay—and headed toward a store in which plucked and drawn chickens, their feet tied with string, hung in the win-dow as a sign they were kosher.

Rebekah stuffed the produce in the large market basket they had borrowed from Anna and hurried after her mother.

"Shopping here is not that hard," Leah said and chuckled. "I was so afraid everyone would be speak-ing English."

"Mama, you won't do all your shopping here," Rebekah said. "There are other stores in which peo-ple *will* speak English."

Leah gave a toss of one hand. "There are enough shops in this place where people speak the language I speak. Why should I struggle to learn a language that is hard for me to learn?"

"English is the language of this country, Mama," Rebekah protested. "Since we are going to live here, you'll want to learn the language."

"Yiddish is the language I know," Leah insisted. She briskly stepped ahead, entered the shop with the chickens in the window, and—with confidence—launched into a discussion in Yiddish. She was obviously pleased when the butcher understood her and replied with a smile.

Rebekah fought back her irritation, reminding herself that her family had been in the United States only a short while, and her mother was still afraid of the differences in their way of living.

Rebekah glanced around the shop at the women who dressed exactly as they had in their former countries. This wasn't what Rebekah wanted. She thought of the women she had seen wearing hats and fitted skirts and nipped-in jackets. Was that what university students wore? She realized she hadn't left her country to come to a new one and follow the old ways.

By ten that night a motley collection of furniture and equipment had been delivered to the Levinskys' flat. Lumpy, plush-upholstered, horsehair-stuffed sofas and chairs; hard, straight-backed wooden chairs; a cutting table; sewing tables; and three sewing machines were in place in the living room. On the table were piled spools of black thread, scissors, pins, and the precut pieces that would be sewn together for the boys' pants. A badly weathered armoire in which to hang clothes and a wooden bedstead had been put into each of the two bedrooms, and rope lacings had been strung between the planked sides of the beds to support their thin mattresses of cotton batting.

"I wish I had my feather bed," Sofia murmured.

"Be glad for what you *do* have," Leah told her. "Your brothers will have to sleep on the sofas."

Uncle Avir burst in to wish them a good night's rest and gave them an alarm clock.

"There will be no charge for the clock," Avir said, proud of his generosity. "If you set it for five, you'll have time to eat breakfast before starting work. I have assigned two of my workers—brothers from Poland—to you from now on. They'll arrive at six each morning, and on the first day they'll make sure you understand the assembly procedure."

"I understand what you told me," Elias said, "but I have a suggestion." He held up two of the pieces that would be joined to make a pair of pants. "The seams will lie flatter and hold much longer if we sew double French seams instead of single, unfinished seams."

"Nonsense! French seams would be a waste of time and money!" Avir said.

"I am a tailor, Avir," Elias answered. "I have always done careful, excellent work that I could be proud of. My customers have always been satisfied."

"In this case your customer is only a merchandiser who will sell these pants in his stores. *He* wants a profit, and *we* want a profit. And as far as the boys who wear these pants, they'll never be able to tell you if they're satisfied or not, because you'll never see them. It's important that you do things as I've explained, Elias, so we can finish the order by the end of the week. We won't be paid until after the work is done. Do you understand?"

Elias nodded, and Avir left them with another wish to sleep well.

"I am a tailor," Elias murmured, as though he were speaking to himself, "not someone who carelessly stitches a cheap pair of pants. I have always enjoyed working with fabrics of quality. *Avir* is the one who doesn't understand." He studied the rough material that was still in his hands, and his face twisted into a look of disgust.

Long after Rebekah had spread a pair of Leah's feather comforters on one of the mattresses, tucked Sofia in between them, and climbed in next to her, she thought of what her father had said. *None of us really understands any of the others,* she thought. *At least, no one understands me and what I want.*

But she remembered that somewhere in New York City there *was* someone who had understood. Aaron Mirsch. She and Aaron had promised each other to work to make their wishes come true. Rebekah crooked the little finger of her right hand and could almost feel the pressure of Aaron's finger against it.

"All right, Aaron," Rebekah whispered into her pillow. "If there's a way, I'm going to find it."

CHAPTER FIFTEEN

❖ ❖ ❖

THE loud jangling of the alarm in her parents' room woke Rebekah, and she staggered out of bed, dressing quickly. In the dim early morning light, she took her turn at using the privy in the alley in back of the house and washing her face and hands in the basin Leah had set up at one end of the kitchen.

Her father and brothers said the prayers before eating and Leah served the family a breakfast of boiled eggs, sliced bread, and coffee. By the time Avir's workers—both slight, stoop-shouldered young men—knocked at their door at six o'clock, Rebekah and her family were ready to work.

At eight o'clock, about fifteen minutes after Jacob had left for his yeshiva, Avir came in smiling and nodding as he gazed about the room and found the others hard at work. But his glance stopped at Sofia, who was neatly dressed and ready for school, her hair drawn back tightly and tucked under a fresh white kerchief. "You . . . little Sofia," he said. "You need a job, too. Are you strong enough to carry home a box filled with black buttons from a shop on Broadway?"

Leah shook her head, not looking up from the

seams she was pressing. "Sofia is only eight, Avir," she stated firmly. "If you had children you'd know that she is much too young to go about this city by herself. Besides, Sofia is going to public school."

Avir's eyes widened in amazement. "Public school? What is this? You have debts. You have rent to pay and food to buy. Sofia can wait until next fall to enter school, and right now there are many jobs small fingers can do."

"Avir," Elias answered, "we have talked this over and decided. We will get the pants made on time. We do not need Sofia's help."

Rebekah silently laid aside a waistband on which she had been doing a row of tiny finishing stitches. She stood, pulled on her jacket, and tied her kerchief over her hair. "Give me the name of the button shop and tell me what you need, Uncle Avir," she said. "I'll bring the box back to you."

"I don't want to take you away from the job you have here," he said, "but the boy who usually runs my errands is home ill. I had thought that little Sofia . . ."

"I'll hurry," Rebekah assured him.

He gave directions to the shop and handed her a slip of paper with the address and order written on it. Rebekah shoved it into her pocket and reached for Sofia's hand.

The school was only a few blocks away. It was an imposing building with thick, round columns on each side of the stairway that led to the front door. With a mingled sense of excitement and jealousy, Rebekah guided her sister up the stairs and into the cool hallway. If only *she* had been given the chance to attend a school like this one!

Rebekah found the main office and registered Sofia, then followed directions to the classroom where Sofia would study. Sofia hung on Rebekah's arm, pulling back. "I don't want to go to school," Sofia complained in Yiddish. "I don't know anyone here. I can hardly speak English. I want to go home."

"Sofia! You must be joking! This is a wonderful opportunity for you," Rebekah told her.

"I want to go home," Sofia insisted, and her eyes filled with tears.

Rebekah knew she should be patient, but all she could feel was anger that Sofia was rejecting what Rebekah wanted and couldn't have. "Behave yourself," she snapped and gave Sofia a tug. "You're going to school, and that's that."

Sofia burst into loud wails.

The door to the classroom suddenly opened, and a teacher, who was young and almost as blond as Kristin, looked down at Rebekah and Sofia and smiled. "Do you speak English?" she asked.

Sofia, startled into silence, hid behind Rebekah's legs and held on tightly.

Embarrassed, Rebekah switched to the English language. "Yes, we do," she answered.

"Good!" the teacher said. "So many of the children speak only Yiddish. I'm glad to have this child in my class. My name is Miss Albert."

Rebekah introduced herself and her sister as she struggled to release herself from Sofia's grip.

"Everybody will speak English, and I don't want to speak English," Sofia insisted.

"That's not true, Sofia. Miss Albert said many of the children speak Yiddish."

"I don't believe her," Sofia mumbled and made another grab for Rebekah's legs.

But there was sudden laughter as two girls close to Sofia's age burst into the hall in a game of tag. "You can't catch me!" one of them shouted in Yiddish.

Sofia raised her head and stared at them.

"They speak Yiddish. You see?" Rebekah said.

"Miriam! Gilah! Come here. We have a new student," Miss Albert said. She smiled again at Rebekah, then took Sofia's hand and ushered the three little girls into the classroom.

Rebekah walked down the hall, opened the heavy front door, and hurried down the steps. She thought about Miss Albert's clothes and kind voice. What a wonderful thing to see a woman work as a teacher. She paused, taking deep breaths, as she fought back a burning resentment, but soon gave an impatient shake of her head. Enough feeling sorry for herself. There was work to do. The button shop on Broadway was many blocks away, and she had promised Uncle Avir she would hurry.

Rebekah turned to the right, striding briskly, until she realized that this was not the way she had come. A woman leaned from an upstairs window and called to another, and Rebekah didn't understand the language they were speaking.

Nessin had told them the city was divided. Jewish ... Italians ... Irish ... What had she blundered into? Nessin had been beaten! What would happen to her?

Rebekah turned and began to run, terror blinding her. She dashed across a street, narrowly missing being struck by a heavy cart. She stumbled over a curb—*Which way? Which way?*—and ran toward the right, dodging startled pedestrians.

Had she come this way? Around the next corner Rebekah flew, colliding with a large, solidly built man. As he grabbed her shoulders to steady her, Rebekah could see his dark blue uniform, cap, and badge. He was not a soldier like in Russia. He was a policeman!

Rebekah squeezed her eyelids shut and waited in fear for what would happen next. She knew it was best never to attract attention. It was told that if you were arrested by the Russian police, you might never be seen again.

A hearty voice asked, "Are you all right, young lady?"

Rebekah realized that the policeman's English sounded much the same as her friend Rose's. Could he be Irish? She tried not to be frightened. "I guess I'm all right," she whispered.

He peered down at her. "Then suppose you tell me why you came bounding around that corner in such a hurry."

"I don't know where I am . . . That is, I'm supposed to hurry, but I can't find . . ." Rebekah stopped for breath and added, "I didn't mean to run into you. I'm sorry."

"No harm done," he said and smiled. "It seems to be that you're lost. If you tell me where you're trying to go, I'll be glad to give you directions."

Silently, Rebekah held out the slip of paper to him, and he nodded. "You're headed in the right direction. Now keep going straight, and four blocks from here you'll find Broadway, that's the wide street. Then it's just a simple matter of turning to the right. The shop should be only five or six blocks farther."

"Thank you," Rebekah murmured.

He touched the brim of his cap before he strolled on. Rebekah gave such a loud sigh of relief she hoped he hadn't heard it. The police in the United States were nothing at all like the police in Russia. She calmed herself and carefully followed the officer's directions. Soon she came to Broadway, with its heavy cart and buggy traffic, clopping horses, and hurrying, pushing crowds of people. Where were all the people going? Everyone seemed to be in such a rush.

She noticed young women wearing bright coats and hats and wondered what kind of life these women led. *Could they be students? Was there a university nearby?*

Rebekah's attention was drawn to the large window on the ground floor in the building she was passing. She stopped and stared. The window was decorated like a little room, and behind the glass stood two female mannequins dressed in elegant outfits. Rebekah pressed her nose to the glass, enchanted by the elegant wine-colored coat with a full skirt and narrow waist. It reminded her of the coats she had seen on first-class passengers on the ship. This coat was decorated with black braid that was stitched down the front and around the hem. The collar was black velvet, and gold buttons fastened the coat and sleeves.

She sighed in admiration, then she noticed that the braid was machine stitched in a single line down the center, its edges curling away from the fabric behind it. Papa would never have turned out a coat with such poor quality stitching. Papa's tiny hand stitches would have made that braid lie flat.

With a shrug, Rebekah turned away and walked briskly down Broadway, passing a door over which hung a neatly painted sign on which was lettered: HEBREW IMMIGRANT AID SOCIETY.

So this is where the office was! She peeked into the window and saw a large, comfortable room inside. Maybe she could stop in, just for a minute . . . only to say thank you again. While she was there, she could ask about the evening classes and find out if girls were allowed to enroll.

But she had promised Uncle Avir that she'd hurry. Rebekah walked on by until she reached the button shop, opened the door, and stepped inside.

As a young clerk behind the counter unfolded his long legs from the equally long legs of a high stool and took the slip of paper from her, Rebekah stared around the room in amazement. Fastened to cards and pinned around the walls were buttons of every type, color, and size. She reached out a finger to stroke a smooth, gold-toned button, elegant enough to decorate a woman's expensive, fine suit.

"Are all these buttons for sale?" she asked in awe.

The clerk bent to search for a box under the counter, so his words were muffled. "That's what they're here for," he said in English that obviously had very little accent.

"The gold buttons . . . How much do they cost?"

The clerk stood, thumping a heavy, rectangular box down on the counter, and turned down the corners of his mouth in a wry smile. "More than Avir Levinsky would pay."

Rebekah tried to sound grown-up and haughty.

"Avir Levinsky wouldn't be the one buying those buttons. I would, and I simply asked the price. Will you tell me, please?"

"Those buttons will set you back twenty-five cents each!" He grinned at Rebekah's expression of dismay and shoved the box and a printed pad of order blanks toward her. "Sign here," he said, "and I'll give you the buttons Mr. Levinsky ordered."

But Rebekah had spotted something else—an array of thickly stuffed envelopes with pictures on them of women's suits, dresses, and coats. "What are these?" she asked.

"Patterns," he said.

Rebekah peeked into the open top of the envelope where she saw folds of soft, thin paper. "Do you mean these are paper patterns to lay on cloth when cutting out a garment?" She thought of the thick, rough paper her father had always used.

"The very same," he said. "Made by McCall's, and fifteen cents apiece." His eyes were mocking as he added, "Can I sell you one? Along with the gold buttons?"

"Yes," Rebekah answered slowly as an idea began to grow in her mind. She met his teasing smile and added, "Not right now, but someday."

She signed the order, put a copy of it in her pocket, and hoisted the box filled with buttons to one hip. But at the door she stopped and asked, "Maybe you could tell me, how do women students dress in this country?"

His grin became broader. "You want gold buttons and a degree from Columbia University?" he said, almost laughing but without malice.

"Columbia University—is in New York City? Where girls can be students?"

"Right uptown." He fished through the pattern box and pulled one out, holding up the picture so Rebekah could see it. In the drawing a young woman was dressed in a white, long-sleeved blouse and a skirt that fit snugly over the hips and fell in graceful folds. On the woman's head was a hat like those Rebekah had seen in the store windows. Except for the hat, the outfit looked like the one Sofia's teacher was wearing. "Students dress simply," the clerk said good-naturedly. "If you've got fifteen cents the pattern is yours."

"Later," Rebekah told him. "I'll be back."

She began the trip home, but as she passed the door of the HIAS office, she stopped. *What could one moment hurt?* she thought.

CHAPTER SIXTEEN

❖ ❖ ❖

WHEN Rebekah entered the HIAS office she stood quietly, trying to catch her breath, watching as a woman with gray hair and a pleasant smile came to greet her.

"My family has just arrived in the United States, and my brother Nessin is going to study in your evening classes," Rebekah blurted out, "but I need to know if girls are allowed to take the classes, too?"

"Sit down, dear," the woman said. "First tell me your name."

"Rebekah Levinsky," Rebekah said, "but I haven't got time to sit down."

The woman smiled again. "My name is Gussie Meyer. I'm pleased to meet you, Rebekah, and I'm impressed that you speak English so well."

"There is so much I want to ask you," Rebekah told her, "but my uncle wants me to hurry back with this box of buttons, so all I can ask right now is, are girls allowed to take the evening classes?"

"Of course," Mrs. Meyer answered.

In spite of the fact that Rebekah had received the answer she'd wanted, she was amazed. "You really don't believe that education is wasted on a girl?"

"I certainly do not!"

"To have an education is my dream," Rebekah confessed. "This is a surprising country. In spite of the terrible way people have to live, there are rewards. Is it true that in some of the Western states women can vote?"

"Yes, in Wyoming, Colorado, Utah, and Idaho." Mrs. Meyer's eyes glowed as brightly as candles. "If the hard work put in by all of us suffragettes pays off, women in every one of the forty-eight states will someday have the vote!"

"Even in New York?"

"In New York and in every state."

They laughed together, and Mrs. Meyer asked, "Would you like to sign up now for one of our classes, Rebekah?"

"I can't. Not yet," Rebekah answered and reluctantly began to edge toward the door. "For a while I'll have to work with my parents to help pay the debt we owe my uncle. When that is paid off, and we have saved enough money to send for my grandfather, then I think my father and mother will be more willing to listen to my reasons for getting an education."

"Where do you work?"

"In our home."

"Sewing?"

"Yes. I'm a finisher. I do the hand stitches on garments." Rebekah shifted the box, which gave a muted rattle. "I was supposed to hurry back with these buttons. I've taken far too long."

"Have other people been hired to work with your family?"

"Yes." Rebekah could tell from Mrs. Meyer's expression that she knew all about sweatshops. Rebekah was embarrassed.

"Not everyone in New York City lives in such crowded conditions, Rebekah," Mrs. Meyer told her. "I hope your family will soon repay the debt and your father will find another job and be able to move the family to a larger apartment in a quieter neighborhood."

"Where would a quieter neighborhood be?" Rebekah asked in surprise. All she had seen in New York City were crowded, noisy neighborhoods.

"My parents came from Germany. We started out living on the Lower East Side. My father was a peddler," Mrs. Meyer said. "But they prospered, and eventually my father established a large dry goods store. They moved to the Upper East Side. I hope your family will prosper, too, and you will attend our classes."

"Thank you," Rebekah said. With new energy, her mind racing almost as fast as her feet, Rebekah strode briskly for the entire long walk back to the flat.

That night, after work had ceased, Rebekah told her father what she had seen at the button shop.

"Papa, you could use those patterns to tailor elegant suits and coats for women. Yours would have hand-finished seams and hidden stitches and beautiful detailing."

"If only I could, Rebekah," her father replied.

"You can, Papa. We need to put aside a few pennies a week, but it will add up. When we have enough you can buy a pattern—oh, you should see those beautiful patterns!—and a fine piece of wool, and the trimmings, and make a lovely coat."

Her mother broke in. "But what could he do with this coat? Sell it on Hester Street? He wouldn't earn enough to pay back what it would cost to make. Be practical, Rebekah."

"Mama, there are big clothing stores here," Rebekah continued, and she told about the mannequins she'd seen. "Papa could take the coat to show to the owners of that store and to others. Surely, they'd be interested in clothes that were beautifully tailored. They'd want to sell that coat for him at a good profit, and they'd probably hire him to tailor more coats."

Elias looked hopeful, but he said, "I don't know, Rebekah. We are strangers in this country, and we don't know how things like this are done."

She ran around to face him, kneeling on the floor and clasping his hands. "Maybe someone at the Hebrew Immigrant Aid Society could tell us."

"Maybe in the future we can discuss this possibility," Elias said, "but in the present we have our responsibility to pay back Avir."

In the future. We'll discuss a good tailoring job in the future. We'll talk about the possibility of your schooling, Rebekah, in the future. Did everything have to wait? "Papa," Rebekah complained.

But Leah interrupted. "No more talk tonight," she said. "Look how your father's head is hurting."

"Did I say my head is hurting?"

"I can tell when your head is hurting. Now . . . off to bed, everyone. We have to wake up very early, and we all need our sleep."

*　　*　　*

138

The family quickly adjusted to the routine Avir had set, beginning work each day at six and continuing until nine at night in order to keep on schedule. Cloth scraps lay everywhere, and a dusting of black lint covered everyone and everything in the room.

The brisk walks Rebekah took as she escorted Sofia to and from school became the highlights of Rebekah's days; for a short time she escaped the heat and drudgery of the sweatshop. She encouraged Sofia to read her lessons out loud while Rebekah hand stitched garments, praising her use of English, helping her with words that were difficult. *This is what Mordecai would have done,* Rebekah told herself. *This is what a teacher would do.*

Rebekah knew she should rejoice for Nessin, who left work in the early evening in order to be on time for his classes, but each time he left the house she fought back a pang of bitterness, wishing that *she* were the one who was going to school. This was supposed to be a land of freedom, yet for her it was not.

On Friday, soon after the first half of the order of boys' pants had been picked up, wrapped, and taken away to be delivered to the manufacturer, Anna—who was usually too busy to visit them—came by to share their noon meal.

"Anna," Leah said, "the Shabbas meal tomorrow noon will be ours to share with you and Avir to thank you for your help."

Anna looked startled, then her gaze slid away. "We have no time to keep Shabbas, Leah. Avir doesn't even go to synagogue much."

Rebekah was as shocked as her mother. How could they not keep Shabbas, the day of rest?

"Anna! There is no question about keeping Shabbas!" Leah cried out.

Anna still didn't meet her sister-in-law's eyes as she explained, "The sewing shops operate seven days a week. They have to. If our workers were not paid for seven days, they would leave us and work for someone else. And how could we possibly close down early on Friday? It is not just the blessing and the lighting of candles twenty minutes before sundown. It's all that must be done to prepare beforehand. You know it takes time to clean the house and do the ritual washing." Her tone became pleading as she continued. "Avir has been able to get some large orders, but the companies want the garments to be completed quickly. The sooner they are ready, the sooner they can be sold. Don't you see, Leah? This is the way it must be, at least for now."

"For you and Avir it can be this way, if this is what you want to do with your life, but why should it be that way for us?"

Avir's voice startled Leah as he spoke from the doorway. "It must be that way for you as well. It is exactly as Anna has explained. Merchants are always in a hurry to have their orders filled. If we do not work seven days, as the others do, then we will get *none* of the orders and we will starve."

"Papa?" Jacob whispered.

Elias, who had remained silent, twisted in his chair. "Sit down, Avir, and we will talk," he finally said.

As soon as his brother was seated Elias stated firmly, "We have always kept Shabbas. You and Anna—in Russia you kept Shabbas. It is our way and our obligation."

Avir looked down at his hands. "I would like to again," he said, "but you have to understand, Elias, that many, many people are coming to this country. There are more people than there are jobs. When Anna and I first came there were many days we went hungry. I could never explain to you how frightened we were!"

"You wrote that you were doing well," Leah broke in.

Avir and Anna looked at each other. Anna's face reddened with embarrassment, but Avir shrugged. "You warned us not to go. Father thought we were wrong to leave Russia."

"The rebbes who warned against going seem to have been right in your case," Elias interrupted.

Avir impatiently shook his head. "We haven't lost our faith. We were forced to adapt to the situation in this country. Listen to me, Elias. We were hungry. We could have starved, but I was fortunate to get a job in a sweatshop, while Anna . . ." He looked down at the floor. "For a while Anna scrubbed floors in an office building. It was honest work, but we were not happy. How could we be?"

"But we saved our money," Anna said, and she put a consoling hand on her husband's arm. "And Avir was able to buy sewing machines and begin his own shop. We are doing well, now. We are able to give employment to others. We have been able to help you. We are not heathen, but our views are different now. We're more American."

"By working seven days a week," Elias said, "by not keeping Shabbas you have become American? Are there no days of rest and respect?"

Avir jumped to his feet and excitedly waved his

arms. "We are *here* in a free country!" he cried. "And *you* are here! We no longer have to be afraid for our lives just because we are Jews. Here Jews live next to Christians without killing each other. What more do you want, Elias!"

"I want my family to keep Shabbas," Elias answered.

"You praise God every day through your prayers."

"Avir," Elias said quietly, "Shabbas is our testimony of hope. What would life be without hope?"

Avir sighed and dropped back into the chair. "Did you keep Shabbas on the boat to America? No, because of the circumstances you did not," he said. "Again, it is the circumstances of how we must work that prevents us from keeping Shabbas. Someday we will keep it again, but if we worked only five and a half days, instead of seven, it would take us longer to complete our work, and the manufacturers would stop giving us orders. We would starve, Elias."

"What of those who work in the factories?" Elias asked, but Avir shook his head in frustration.

"The factory workers keep almost the same hours and earn much less than we do. The factories are like death traps—no ventilation, no air or space."

Rebekah knew she should remain silent and allow the adults to settle the problem. A girl, even in the family, had no right to interrupt, but she quietly asked, "Why can't the workers explain to the manufacturers about the importance of Shabbas?"

Avir answered with a hoarse laugh. "The manufacturers know about Shabbas and our other holy days. Do you think they care? All they want is to make money."

"What if all the workers joined together?" Rebekah went on. "If they all refused to work until the working conditions were changed, then wouldn't the manufacturers have to agree?"

"My niece is an organizer and she's only just arrived! I have heard talk of workers organizing," Avir answered, "but it is nothing but talk. Nothing will come of it. Nothing can. With the hordes of people arriving in this country each day, the manufacturers can fire the workers they suspect of causing trouble and hire new workers. But you, Rebekah, must learn your place."

Impatiently dismissing Rebekah, Avir turned to his brother. "I have been fortunate to have my bid accepted for a large order which we will share—two hundred men's coats—and we must work quickly to finish them by the promised date of delivery. You do understand, don't you, Elias? As my brother I ask you to do only what I would do myself."

Rebekah held her breath as she waited for her father's answer. Shabbas, the day of rest. Rebekah loved the Saturday full of prayers, forgiveness, and family closeness. Suddenly she thought of Aaron's family. Was this why they had changed, too?

Finally, Elias raised his head, but he spoke to his family, rather than to Avir. "When our people were enslaved by the Egyptians and forbidden to practice their faith, they kept their covenant with God, and eventually He led them out of bondage. Until we are established here in New York, until we are able to find a new direction in our lives, we will work on Saturday, but we will trust in God to guide us. We will keep our covenant with Him and hope God forgives us this trespass."

Avir let out a sigh of relief and climbed to his feet. "A wise decision," he said.

But Rebekah wondered what was wise anymore.

CHAPTER SEVENTEEN

❖ ❖ ❖

As soon as Avir and Anna had left, Elias told the others, "Work quickly. God knows that in our hearts we have prepared for the welcoming of Shabbas, so we will at least make time for the blessing and prayers."

Rebekah's fingers flew as she stitched, and even the pair of brothers who worked for them were intent on their work, pleased at being included in Elias's plans. When it was time to pick up Sofia, Rebekah ran all the way to the public school and tugged home her reluctant little sister.

Leah had placed on the kitchen table two white candles in her silver candlesticks, loaves of challah covered by an embroidered cloth, and the kiddush cup, but all in the room were bent over their tasks, and Rebekah immediately went back to work.

No one spoke during working hours. There wasn't time for social conversation, so Rebekah had paid little attention to the workers, aside from returning their polite greetings each morning; but when Elias announced it was time to wash and prepare for the lighting of the candles, Rebekah saw pleasure in their eyes.

They all worked together to tidy the room as well as they could, then used the pitcher and basin to wash the black lint from their arms, necks, and faces. They gathered around the table. Leah covered her hair, then lit the candles as she recited the blessing.

"Shabbat shalom!" Leah said to Rebekah, and the others repeated the greeting to each other.

Elias led the Shabbas psalm, and they joined in singing *Shalom Aleichem.*

Although Rebekah twice saw her mother glance nervously in the direction of Avir's apartment, even Leah soon lost herself in the warmth of Elias's blessings as he held the filled kiddush cup.

After the ritual washing of hands, they sat at the table for the breaking of the challah and the festive meal. By the time the prayers after the meal had been said, Rebekah had heard from Asa and Mischa that they had come from Poland with their wives more than a year before. Mischa and his wife had a ten-month-old baby, and Asa's wife was expecting a child within four months.

"Born in America," Mischa said proudly, and Asa grinned. "Not greenhorns!"

"Born in freedom," Asa said.

This is freedom? Rebekah asked herself, but this was not the time nor the place for rebellious thoughts. She smiled, wished them *mazel,* and went on eating.

Rebekah was thrilled when a little more than a week later a letter arrived from Kristin. Her words were like sunshine, and as she read the news of a new life, Kristin's energy and enthusiasm gave her hope.

"Father bought a farm, complete with a farmhouse, near the little community of Scandia. I have to admit that the countryside is beautiful and looks very much like Sweden. This part of the country is like being home since everyone around here speaks Swedish and decorates their houses the way they did in Sweden. My mother says it's easier to be around our own kind.

"Minnesota reminds me so much of home. At first I thought I would die from being homesick, but then a wonderful thing happened. I met a woman from Minneapolis. You should see the wonderful cities of Minneapolis and St. Paul! We saw the cities mostly from the train, but they're exciting. I can't wait to return someday and explore them!

"Enough about the cities. Sigrid Larson is the woman I've met and she is unique. She is in Scandia visiting her sister. My father doesn't like her because she says women can do as many things as men."

Kristin ended her letter, "Oh, how I miss you, Rebekah! Write to me! Tell me what you're doing! I haven't met any girls our age I like as much as you. Write soon!"

Rebekah wanted to write. She missed Kristin and Rose, too. But Kristin lived in a beautiful town, much like the one she'd left in her own home country. Rebekah was embarrassed to tell her about New York's Lower East Side and the kind of work her family had to do in order to survive. Before Rebekah fell asleep each night she'd begin to compose letters in her mind, only to toss and groan and discard each miserable attempt.

Rebekah grew more and more impatient at the drudgery of her work, which caused an ache that spread from her lower back through her shoulders and into her neck. Toward evening her eyes burned and her vision blurred as she plied her needle in and out of the rough fabric with tiny, almost invisible stitches. Twice she brought up the topic of schooling to her mother, but on both occasions Leah sighed loudly and begged Rebekah to wait to even begin to think about such a thing.

"There is so much we must adjust to," Leah said, but her explanation didn't satisfy Rebekah. Like so many of the other women who were crowded into this neighborhood, Leah wasn't making much of an attempt to try to learn English. Elias firmly refused to listen again to Rebekah's hope that he would break away from Avir's sweatshop and try to find work as a tailor of quality garments.

"This is not the time," he had told her. "We are not ready yet to make such a drastic change."

"But *when* will we be?" Rebekah implored.

Elias's voice was gentle but firm. "Your grandfather must be sent for, we must pay back our debt to Avir, and we must support your brothers' studies—especially Jacob's—so they can make us proud."

Rebekah saw her dream fading, like the morning mists that had drifted so briefly over the sea. She ached with despair. If only her grandfather were there. And where was Aaron? Had he forgotten her already? Why hadn't he come to see her? Was he caught in a trap like Rebekah's—one from which he could find no escape? Would they both be condemned to lives of drudgery?

The Levinskys had lived in New York City almost two months before a letter dated mid-June arrived from Mordecai. The sewing temporarily halted as Elias read the letter aloud.

In his fine, spidery handwriting Mordecai reported that he had arrived safely in London. His cousin Samuel had not only taken him in, but had found him work with a book publisher who was in need of a Russian translator. The publisher was pleased with Mordecai's work, and Mordecai was pleased with his new job.

"The pay is not much above what I consider to be a fair weekly contribution to Samuel's household," Mordecai wrote, "but my needs are few, and I am thankful I'm able to save toward my next passage to the United States."

Mordecai sent his love to each member of the family with a note for each one. To Rebekah he had written, "Through your daily work and prayers, I hope you keep your dreams in mind. Someday they will come true and I hope to be in the United States to see them happen."

As tears flooded her eyes, Rebekah thought, *Grandfather doesn't know what it's like here. How can I keep my dreams in mind when no one will listen to me?*

During the rest of the day, as Rebekah worked, her grandfather's words kept returning.

That night, before she went to bed, Rebekah wrote to Mordecai, pouring out all the frustration she felt at the horrible life they had to lead and at her parents, who seemed content to follow this endless path forever. "What can I do, Grandfather?" she wrote, hoping with all her heart that Mordecai would have the answer.

Rebekah sealed the letter, and in the morning

when she took Sofia to school, she mailed it. It wasn't hard to convince her father to part with the money for postage, but she knew that every penny counted.

She had been told how to find the post office by the school clerk, and she paid careful attention to the streets she had to cross. Remembering her earlier experiences, Rebekah was determined never to become lost again.

She left the post office and strode to the corner, where she stopped, waiting for a large, heavily loaded horse-drawn dray to pass.

"Please help me! Miss! Oh, Miss! Help me!" a voice called in Yiddish.

Rebekah whirled toward the whispery voice and saw a woman clutching a husky baby boy. The woman's face was white, and she struggled to focus her eyes, frantically reaching out toward Rebekah.

Rebekah took the baby, then with her right hand she firmly gripped the woman's shoulder—leading, supporting, and pushing her toward the steps of a nearby building.

"Sit here!" Rebekah said. "Put your head between your knees." She kept her eyes on the woman but felt the eyes of the little boy silently study her.

"I'm sorry. For a moment I felt faint," the woman mumbled in Yiddish, her head nearly buried in the folds of her faded and patched skirt. Slowly, she raised herself to a sitting position and leaned against the wrought-iron railing.

Relieved that a little color was coming back into the woman's face, Rebekah asked, "Are you hungry?" She fingered the two pennies left in her pocket.

"No. It's not hunger," the woman said, and she

glanced away, gently resting a hand on her slightly rounded abdomen.

"Where do you live?" Rebekah asked. "Are you near your home?"

"Please could you walk with me a short way? Just to the Henry Street Settlement?"

Rebekah's look must have revealed her ignorance, so the woman explained, "That's the place Lillian Wald set up to help Jewish immigrants. Last winter, when my boy ran a fever, her nurses gave him good care."

"The Henry Street Settlement is a hospital?"

"No. It's a clinic. Miss Wald is a nurse who comes from a wealthy family. They are German Jews not Russians, but she and her nurses live in the Lower East Side so they can help poor people. Each day her clinic does hundreds of *mitzvahs*." For the first time the woman smiled, and Rebekah could see a gap at each side of her mouth where she'd lost a few teeth. "What you are doing for me is a *mitzvah*, as well, and I thank you."

She struggled to her feet, took a long, deep breath, and led the way to the Henry Street Settlement. Rebekah carefully took notice of landmarks: the house with its brown paint peeling, a flower pot in a third-story window, a sign offering room and board tacked to a front-door post. A new street, a new adventure.

Each day I'll go home a different way. I'll travel a different street, Rebekah promised herself.

She would have to work late to make up the tasks she was neglecting, but she knew her parents would agree that the performance of a good deed was of the highest importance.

Inside the waiting room of the settlement were seated many women, most of them with babies and young children. There was a great deal of activity in the crowded room, as a line of women waited to register at a desk while nurses in starched white dresses arrived and departed, leading patients to other areas of the building.

Rebekah was startled when a smartly dressed woman in a tailored blue suit suddenly stepped up to her and asked, "Have you registered your baby yet?"

"Baby? Oh, he's not mine," Rebekah answered. "I'm holding him for his mother."

The woman smiled and stepped aside to greet a man who was carrying a large box filled with neatly folded items of clothing. On top of the box, immediately catching Rebekah's attention, rested a beautiful and simple black straw hat with a flat round brim and a wide white ribbon tied around the crown. It wasn't a fancy hat with feathers or flowers or veils—the kind of hat a mature woman would admire. It was a hat like some of those Rebekah had seen on the street, perfect for a young woman—like herself.

The man carried the box into another room, and Rebekah fingered the pennies in her pocket again. The clothing was obviously used. She doubted it was for the nurses who worked at the Settlement. Maybe it was for the patients and their families. Maybe it was for sale. If so, how much would a hat like that cost? The used-hat peddlers on Hester Street tried to sell their hats for a quarter apiece, but often accepted much less. But she had only two cents, and surely a beautiful hat like that would cost much more.

Rebekah cautioned herself to forget the hat, but when the woman in the blue suit returned to the waiting room, Rebekah shifted the little boy to one hip and hurried toward her. "The clothes the man just brought—are they for sale?"

"For sale?" The woman shook her head. "No. We are a nursing clinic, but occasionally someone wants to donate clothing to those in need and, not knowing where else to take it, brings it here."

"Oh," Rebekah said. "The hat on top of the box . . . the beautiful hat . . . I hoped it might be for sale."

At that moment the mother of the baby arrived and swept her child into her arms. "Thank you for helping me," she said to Rebekah. "You don't know how frightened I was. I wish for you a lifetime of blessings." She turned and hurried toward a nurse who was waiting.

The woman in the suit smiled at Rebekah and said, "With the blessings should go a pretty hat." She stepped back and studied Rebekah's plain brown dress. "A pretty girl like you who might want to be in fashion should wear the hat with a shirtwaist and skirt."

"But I don't . . ."

"It's quite likely I can give you what you deserve, just wait a moment."

Rebekah found herself back on the street holding a paper-wrapped bundle. She held it carefully, thrilled to own a white cotton shirtwaist, a black serge fitted skirt, and the beautiful straw hat. When she got home, instead of going to the workroom, she tucked the bundle into the bottom of the armoire—a secret only she would know. She didn't want her mother objecting. She'd wait to wear the clothes when it was the proper time . . . when she, Rebekah Levinsky, was a student.

Giddy with happiness, Rebekah smiled and felt a new surge of hope.

CHAPTER EIGHTEEN

❖ ❖ ❖

ADDING to the joy of the day, a letter arrived from Rose. Rebekah read it over and over again.

"And what has happened to the girl, Rose, who danced in front of everyone?" Leah asked.

Rebekah giggled. "The train ride to Chicago had its problems. Rose routed a robber who was trying to steal her suitcase. She gave him a fine clout on the head while stomping on his toes."

"Ach!" Leah said. "A young girl without protection! What was her uncle thinking of? If her mother only knew ..."

"Rose calls Chicago, 'a monstrous big place.' She's written about seeing her father and brothers again."

"They are in good health, I trust?"

Rebekah folded the letter and returned it to its envelope. "I guess so. Rose's father is a bricklayer, with steady work because so many buildings are being constructed. Her brother Michael has learned the trade of pipe fitter and is doing well. She said her brother John is working in the office of someone called an alderman. It must be a high position because the alderman commands a great deal of respect according to Rose. As a favor to John his boss was able to get Rose a job as a sales clerk. She works in a small dry goods store and is happy about that. She had been so sure that the only position she could get would be what most Irish girls in Chicago settle for—a maid for rich people. Rose said their father is so proud of John he can't stop bragging about him."

"I'm glad Rose had good news to relate," her mother said, smiling.

Rebekah didn't repeat to her mother what Rose had confided about her brother John: "I know Johnny well, and I remember that always, if mischief was afoot, he was not only involved in it, but he got me in trouble, too. My father doesn't seem to see that Johnny keeps late hours, coming and going no one knows where, and I suspect that once again my brother has been drawn toward the mischief. I just hope I'm wrong."

Rebekah walked new streets, trying to learn more about the vast city of New York, but the blocks in her Lower East Side neighborhood were much the same. Windows in the crowded brick and wooden buildings had been thrown open in the warm weather, and from them came the constant buzz and hum of the machines. Small children played in the streets, but the gray patina of poverty was everywhere.

As week followed week, and Rebekah ventured farther from her path to and from Sofia's school, she had to run to keep from losing time at work. One afternoon Rebekah stopped abruptly as she heard the clear notes of a flute drifting from a window three stories over her head.

"Aaron?" she whispered, and ran eagerly up the

stairs to the third floor, not stopping until she reached a door on which was painted LEPSKI'S SCHOOL OF MUSIC.

She paused to catch her breath, then knocked timidly.

The flute music continued, so she knocked again, this time more loudly.

The music stopped. Rebekah could hear footsteps stomping across a bare wooden floor, and the door swung open. A heavyset, bushy-bearded man, who was carrying a flute, stared down at her. "You've come to see about lessons?" he asked.

"N—No," Rebekah stammered. "I'm looking for someone named Aaron Mirsch. I thought the flute . . . that is, his music . . ."

"I know of no one named Aaron Mirsch," the man said and impatiently shut the door.

Slowly, Rebekah descended the stairs, her disappointment as heavy as a stone in her stomach. It had been several months since she and Aaron had arrived in the United States. "I'll show up on your doorstep," Aaron had promised, but Rebekah was afraid that this promise, like those they had made to each other about their future goals, might never be kept. Because of her work she couldn't meet people her age. Aaron was her only friend. Would she never see him again?

Rebekah and Sofia arrived home to find that work had stopped. Their mother and aunt wept in each other's arms, and Elias's eyes were red and puffy. Avir sobbed loudly into a handkerchief.

Nessin, whose head had been resting on the

157

kitchen table, looked up at Rebekah with stricken eyes.

"What is it?" Rebekah managed to ask, but she knew. She knew!

Leah reached out to enfold her daughters in her arms. "Oh, Rebekah," she sobbed. "The worst of news! Your Grandfather Mordecai—*ohav shalom!*—has died."

Rebekah felt herself plunging into a dark pit, but she clung to her mother and fought to remain conscious. "It can't be true!" she cried. "Grandfather is coming to join us! As soon as we save enough money! Grandfather can't die! No! No! I don't believe it!"

Leah helped Rebekah into a chair and handed her a glass of water. Gently she removed Rebekah's kerchief and smoothed back her hair as she said, "It's true. Samuel has written to inform us."

Sofia began to wail. Rebekah wrapped her arms around her little sister, and they wept together.

Finally, when her tears had become only dry sobs, Rebekah slumped, exhausted, in her chair. "Mama, tell me, how did Grandfather die?" she asked.

"Quietly, in his sleep," Leah answered. "He had not been ill. He didn't suffer. For this we can be thankful."

Rebekah didn't feel thankful. She was ashamed of herself, but she was furious. Mordecai had promised to come. She needed him, and he had left her.

Leah placed an envelope into Rebekah's hand, but Rebekah shook her head angrily and tried to return it. "I don't want to read it," she said.

"This is not Samuel's letter," Leah told her. "This

is a letter Mordecai had begun writing to you. Samuel was sure you would want to have it."

Clutching the envelope to her chest, Rebekah slowly climbed to her feet. It was hard to move. There was no feeling in her legs or arms, and only a dark, empty hole in her mind. But somehow she made her way to the room she shared with Sofia, sat on the edge of the bed, and opened the letter.

"Your letter to me made me happy and sad," Mordecai had written. "You are impatient with your parents because you are young. You do have a life of promise before you. Your parents, whom I know you love and respect, are more concerned with problems of the present. They are adults, with most of their lives behind them. They willingly left all that they knew in order to make a better life for their children, whose years lie ahead of them. Do not be harsh with your mother and father if they have difficulty adjusting to the ways of the New World. To travel to the United States was a hard decision to make, and it called for courage. You have courage, too, and you can make their arduous journey worthwhile by following your own dreams yet obeying your parents as a daughter must."

"Without your help?" Rebekah whispered. "How can I?"

Loud voices from the kitchen startled her, and she ran toward them, wondering what had happened.

"How can you say that we'll not sit shiva for seven days?" Elias thundered. "Are you out of your mind, Avir? You know that we must mourn our father not for just two days but as is required by Jewish law."

Red patches blotched Avir's face as he shouted

back, "We cannot put life and earnings aside for an entire week. Clothing manufacturers will not patiently wait while we sit and mourn for our father. We have contracts to meet and workers to pay. If we do not meet our deadlines, we will get no more work. We'll lose our homes. We'll be out on the street with no jobs, no money. Do you want your family to starve to death? Our father would understand."

"Our faith . . . our tradition . . ." Elias waved his hands, at a loss for words.

"In the evenings we will meet and pray," Avir went on, his voice dropping to a normal pitch. "You and I will say kaddish as we must as respectful sons. Believe me, he will understand. God will understand."

Avir put a hand on his brother's shoulder, his voice heavy with urgency and tears. "And it's important to all of us—to our survival, Elias—that *you* understand. Asa, Mischa, and the people who work for me—would you have them out of a job? Searching with thousands of others for work?"

Asa broke in, his voice cracking as he pleaded, "Elias, you know that my wife is expecting a baby."

In the silence that followed Elias let out a long sigh. "I realize there are others to think of besides ourselves. I am not sure what God is asking of me, but we will do as you say, Avir."

Rebekah turned and ran back to the bedroom, flinging herself on the bed. "Oh, Grandfather! Grandfather, I need you!" she cried aloud, but she knew he would never be there to comfort her. How could she follow her dreams in such a country—a place that had promised her whole family freedom, but little by little took away everything they had held dear?

CHAPTER NINETEEN

❖ ❖ ❖

THE Levinskys worked late, trying to make up for the time they had lost. Angrily Rebekah attacked the cloth she was working on, accidentally jabbing her needle into her finger hard enough to draw blood.

It wasn't fair for Mordecai to die! Rebekah popped her finger into her mouth to take away the pain. Maybe he didn't. Maybe the boat trip, New York—none of this really happened. Maybe it was all a nightmare, and she would wake up to find herself tucked into her soft feather bed at home.

Asa and Mischa had left and an overtired Sofia had been tucked into bed when the sound of footsteps clattering up the stairs startled Rebekah and her parents. They turned toward the door, which Nessin flung open as he ran into the room.

"Oh, it's only Nessin. You frightened us," Rebekah began, but Leah cried out and rushed toward her son.

"You've been fighting again!" she said. "Look at that swollen eye!"

It wasn't just Nessin's right eye, darkening with a spreading bruise, that startled Rebekah.

Nessin didn't try to make excuses. Suddenly, his lower lip curled out, and he whimpered like a small child. "Papa . . . Mama," he said, "there was a gang fight. We had to let them know they couldn't get away with it. And then . . ."

A tear ran down his cheek, and his voice dropped to a whisper. "Someone had a knife. I don't know who it was. One of the Italian boys was stabbed."

Leah gasped, and Elias demanded, "Nessin. Do you know—was the boy killed?"

"I don't think so, but the police came, and . . . Oh, Papa, I ran." He flopped onto the nearest sofa, burrowed his head in his arms, and sobbed.

Leah stared at her son in horror, but Elias laid a hand on Nessin's shoulder and asked, "Do you know who had the knife?"

"No. There were so many boys there."

"How many?"

"About fifty, I think," he mumbled through his tears.

Leah clasped her hands and whispered in terror, "What will we do if the police come here?"

Elias answered. "Nessin will simply tell them what he told us—the truth. The police in this country are not like the police in Russia. They will not take him away."

Nessin stopped crying. He raised his head and wiped his eyes on his coat sleeve.

Furious at her brother, Rebekah asked the question her parents hadn't thought of asking. "How could this have happened to you, Nessin? At this time of night you should be in class."

Nessin hung his head. "I haven't been going to class. I don't care about school. I work so hard all day . . . Don't you see, I need to spend time with my friends." He looked plaintively at Rebekah. "You were born with your nose in a book. I don't expect you to understand. I sew all day, what good will my classes do?"

Rage, frustration, and the pain of losing Mordecai exploded into words as Rebekah grabbed Nessin's shoulders, shaking and berating him. "Nessin! You're a *yold*! You're *meshuga*! Is this all you want for yourself—a life of work in a sweatshop? You have a chance to make something of yourself!"

Although Nessin was stronger than Rebekah, he had a hard time pulling away. "Stop it!" he yelled at her and leaped to his feet.

But Rebekah didn't want to stop. "Are you such a fool that you don't see that there's another way to live? That the only way to escape the sweatshop is with an education?"

"What I do is none of your business," Nessin grumbled.

"It *is* my business! You've been given the chance for an education and turned it down, but I've begged . . . and longed for . . ."

Rebekah's voice broke with a sob, but she shook her head to clear it and snatched up a kerchief that lay on the table, tying it over her hair. "Grandfather told me to follow my dreams," she shouted at him, "and that's what I'm going to do. This isn't a family I know anymore. Everything is different. Well, I'm different, too."

As she put her hand on the doorknob, Leah cried out, "Rebekah! What are you thinking of? You can't go out alone on the streets at night!"

"I must do what must be done, Mama," Rebekah

answered, and she hurried out the door, racing down the stairs.

She ran most of the distance to Broadway, not stopping until she reached the door of the Hebrew Immigrant Aid Society. Through the window she could see the brightly lit office where people clustered in groups, laughing and talking. She was not too late!

Rebekah burst through and shut the door behind her, leaning against it.

An older man with a short, trimmed beard, detached himself from the group nearest the door and said to Rebekah in Yiddish, "I am Stanley Lemann. How may I help you?"

Using all the courage she possessed Rebekah blurted out, "I want to enroll in your classes."

Mr. Lemann nodded. "Very good. I assume you'll want to learn to speak and read English."

Rebekah winced. What a miserable start she had made. In English she said, "I already speak and read English. I want to take all the courses I'll need so that someday I can go to . . . to Columbia University!"

She held her breath, but no one laughed. No one even looked surprised.

"That's an ambitious project," Mr. Lemann said.

Rebekah nodded. "I know it is, but I want an education. I'm willing to work hard to get it."

Mr. Lemann studied Rebekah. Then he said, "Suppose you come in tomorrow night about nine to go over the materials. We'll find out which subjects you'll need to study. Can you be here tomorrow?"

Rebekah took a deep breath. "Yes," she said.

As a young man came up to ask Mr. Lemann a

question, he excused himself and walked with the student toward his desk.

The others in his group returned to their conversations, leaving Rebekah standing alone. She felt awkward and embarrassed, not knowing what to do next.

She glanced at the other students and then her heart stopped. Could it be?

Aaron Mirsch was far across the room, lost in a conversation.

Had Aaron seen her? Rebekah put a hand to her slipping kerchief, feeling loose strands of hair straggling out around it. In panic she thought, *Aaron can't see me like this! I must look like a wild woman!* She turned to escape from the room to the street and bumped straight into the arms of her father.

"Papa!" she cried. "You followed me!"

"It's late," Elias said firmly. "A young girl should not be on the streets alone."

As they walked toward the flat Rebekah said, "I'm sorry, Papa. Please understand why I was so angry. It just seemed so unfair to me that Nessin . . ." She broke off, realizing that her voice had risen. There was no point in becoming upset again.

Elias didn't answer, and Rebekah had to hurry to keep up with his long strides. "Papa," she began again. "I can take classes at the center. Mr. Lemann . . . he said I could enroll."

"Rebekah," Elias interrupted, "we will not talk of this now."

"All right, Papa," Rebekah said quietly, "but I want you to know that I will not give up my dream, no matter how hard it is to reach it."

"Rebekah," Elias warned, and during the rest of the walk they were silent.

In the morning at the kitchen table Rebekah tried to talk to both her parents. "Papa . . . Mama," she began.

But Elias said firmly, "Not now, Rebekah," and gave a quick nod toward Nessin, who drooped with misery.

Why can't we talk? We must discuss Nessin, the gangs, the center, my studies, all of it, Rebekah thought with frustration, but neither of her parents spoke of what had happened the night before.

While the Levinskys were still eating breakfast, Avir came to report that he'd heard in the street that the Italian boy had lived and would soon recover.

"News spreads by neighbors faster than by newspaper," he said, jovial at being the bearer of good news. But his manner changed and he spoke sternly to Nessin. "Come to me if you have nothing better to do with your time than run with street gangs. There is always plenty of work that needs to be done."

"Nessin will be kept busy and out of trouble from now on, believe me," Elias answered.

But Nessin didn't look very happy, and Rebekah's face burned as she thought how happy she would be if she were the one sent to study at night.

Uncle Avir looked as though he had more to say. Whatever it was, Rebekah didn't want to hear it. She hurried to the front room, folding her brothers' quilts and readying the room for work. Through the open windows she thought she heard the gentle trill of a flute, but she kept working. She stopped and listened, then ran to the window and poked her head outside. She looked to her left and to her right and saw no one at first. Then, amid the crowd, she saw him. "Aaron!" she called.

Aaron lowered his flute and smiled up at her. "You ran away last night before I could talk to you," he said.

"Last night," she began, then stopped, blushing, as she remembered how she must have looked and how wildly she had behaved. Last night was best forgotten. "Aaron," she said, "where have you been?"

"Not very far from you. Working in the clothing factory," he said. "I'm on my way there now. At night I study. It is part of what I promised you, Rebekah. I'm making a living and finding a way to build a better life."

"What about your music?" She waited for his answer.

"I have had enormous luck. This country has already been good to me. I've auditioned with a respected flutist," he said, and his smile became shy. "He believes I have enough talent to succeed. He is a Jewish fellow who plays in an orchestra. If I can save enough money I'll begin music lessons next year."

"Oh, Aaron. That's wonderful!" Rebekah cried.

"First, though," he added, "I am learning to speak English. I wanted to surprise you, to make you proud of me."

"I *am* proud of you!" Rebekah said. She smiled and added, "I've missed you, Aaron. I feel as though we have known each other much longer than we actually have."

"And I've missed you," Aaron said. He glanced at

the people who were hurrying past him on the street. "I must go now, or I'll be in trouble at work. I'll see you tonight." He took two steps backward, then called, "Rebekah, your smile is just as beautiful as I remembered it." He turned and ran down the sidewalk.

Rebekah stood, pressing her hands against her chest as a rush of mingled joy and sorrow surged through her body. But what about *her* dream? Aaron had said he would see her later, and she hadn't been able to voice the miserable truth: Her parents wouldn't even talk with her about the classes.

During the day Rebekah stubbornly kept her mind on her work, and that evening she tried to hide the hurt on her face as her father and Nessin washed their hands and faces and put on their hats and coats.

"Rebekah," Elias said, "get ready. I will escort you each night to class."

He gave a pointed look to Nessin, but Rebekah jumped to her feet. "Papa, do you mean it?"

"Of course he means it," her mother said. "He doesn't talk just to hear himself talk. Now, hurry. Wash your face. Brush your hair. Don't keep your father waiting. Be a good girl and do what we want you to do."

Rebekah touched her father's arm, and tears came to her eyes. "You understand," she murmured.

"Not completely," Elias answered. "To us, a good marriage for you with a suitable dowry is still the proper thing to do. But in America our lives have been turned upside down. Nothing is the same. Everything seems strange. It is easy for you young ones to adapt, but much harder for your mother and for me. Of course we prize education above all else, but for our sons. Here it is different. My daughter will make me proud with her education.

"I know your grandfather has already prepared you," he said. "Your mother and I have talked about what your grandfather wanted for you and how he encouraged you to follow your dreams. It's hard for us to understand your dream, but since this is what you want, and since your grandfather wanted it for you, then we will support your decision. We want to do what is right, even though we don't truly understand."

"Oh, Papa," Rebekah said, "Grandfather told me to keep my dreams always in mind, but to be honest with you, I don't think even Grandfather really understood my dream."

She waited, her fingers clasped together so tightly that they hurt. "I will make you proud of me, I promise. You'll never regret this."

Elias slowly pulled his watch from his pocket and glanced at it. "Hurry and get ready, Rebekah," he said, "or you and Nessin are going to be late."

"Oh, Papa! Thank you!" Rebekah shouted and threw her arms around him.

As she combed her hair she thought of Aaron. She couldn't wait to tell him that she'd be studying with him. Life would be better now. America really was a land of hope, and just as she had promised Aaron, nothing was going to stop them from reaching their dreams.

ABOUT ELLIS ISLAND

✧ ✧ ✧

ELLIS ISLAND, called by many the "gateway to America," represents a landmark of America's rich cultural heritage. Four out of ten Americans have family who passed through this important place as immigrants.

From 1892 to 1897 the millions of immigrants who entered the United States through Ellis Island first saw a massive wooden building with a blue slate roof and ornamental towers. In 1897 this structure mysteriously burned to the ground. Fortunately, no one was injured, but thousands of immigration records were lost.

A new building was constructed and opened in 1900—an impressive edifice of red and yellow brick, where during the next ten years more than 6 million people were processed. The majority of these immigrants came from Italy, Russia, and Austria-Hungary; but there were many who came from England, Ireland, Germany, and the Scandinavian countries; and some who came from Canada, the West Indies, Poland, Greece, Portugal, and Armenia.

Entry to the United States at Ellis Island wasn't easy. Immigrants faced examinations and inspections and—because of outbreaks of public fear that these individuals might not be able to support themselves—those in poor health or with physical handicaps were returned to the countries from which they came. The complex and confusing entry to the United States was initially made even more difficult for the immigrants because they often did not know English or understand the value of the dollar.

For many years the Ellis Island buildings were deserted, but in 1980 President Ronald Reagan invited Lee Iacocca, chairman of the Chrysler Corporation, to orchestrate the renovation of both the Ellis Island immigration station and the Statue of Liberty through public donations. Over 20 million people responded with gifts totaling over 300 million dollars. Today Ellis Island is a beautiful museum, preserving the stories of its immigrants for posterity.

Three of my four grandparents were immigrants to this country, so writing the Ellis Island books has been especially meaningful to me.

Joan Lowery Nixon

ABOUT THE AUTHOR

JOAN LOWERY NIXON is the acclaimed author of more than eighty fiction and nonfiction books for children and young adults. She is a three-time winner of the Mystery Writers of America Edgar Award and the recipient of many Children's Choice Awards. Her popular books for young adults include *High Trail to Danger*, and its companion novel, *A Deadly Promise*, the bestselling Orphan Train Quartet, for which she received two Golden Spur Awards, and the Hollywood Daughters trilogy. She is currently working on volumes two and three of the Ellis Island books.

Mrs. Nixon and her husband live in Houston, Texas.